S0-AXT-715

"There it is again. Thumping."

"It's nothing," Jillian said. "Just Aunt Morgana."

David whipped around. "But she's—"

"Yes," Jillian said simply.

"Are you trying to tell me that—"

"She haunts the house. She's probably upset that you're here."

David drew a hard breath. He didn't believe in fortune-telling, tarot cards, casting of the runes or any other such nonsense.

"This house is not haunted," he declared. "I don't believe in ghosts."

She sighed at his stubbornness. "What *do* you believe in?"

"What I can touch." He brought his face closer. "What I can see." His lips coursed the curve of her shoulder, then trailed across her jaw. "What I can taste," he said against her mouth.

Dear Reader,

Happy New Year, and many thanks for the notes and letters you've sent to the authors and editors of Silhouette **Special Edition** over the past twelve months. Although we seldom have time to write individual responses, I'd like to take this opportunity to let you know how much we value all your comments. Your praise and plaudits warm our hearts and give our efforts meaning; your questions and suggestions keep us on our toes as we continually strive to make each of our six monthly Silhouette **Special Edition** novels a truly significant romance-reading event.

Our authors and editors believe you deserve writing of the highest caliber, satisfying novelistic scope, and a profound emotional experience with each book you read. Your letters tell us that you've come to trust Silhouette **Special Edition** to deliver romance fiction of that quality, depth, and sensitivity time and time again. With the advent of the new year, we're renewing a pledge: to do our very best, month after month, edition after edition, to continue bringing you "romance you can believe in."

On behalf of all the authors and editors of Silhouette **Special Edition**,

Thanks again and best wishes,

Leslie Kazanjian,
Senior Editor

P.S. This month, ask your bookseller for *The Forever Rose*, a new historical novel by one of your Silhouette **Special Edition** favorites, Curtiss Ann Matlock—the author has promised "family ties" to her next two contemporary novels, coming this year from Silhouette **Special Edition**!

JENNIFER MIKELS
Stargazer

Silhouette Special Edition

Published by Silhouette Books New York

America's Publisher of Contemporary Romance

SILHOUETTE BOOKS
300 East 42nd St., New York, N.Y. 10017

ISBN: 0-373-09574-0

First Silhouette Books printing January 1990

Printed in the U.S.A.

JENNIFER MIKELS

has been a full-time writer for seven years. She started out an avid fan of historical novels, which eventually led her to contemporary romances, which in turn led her to try her hand at penning her own novels. She quickly found she preferred romance fiction with its happy endings to the technical writing she'd done for a public relations firm. Between writing and raising two teenage boys, the Phoenix-based author has little time left for hobbies, though she does enjoy cross-country skiing and antique shopping with her husband.

KEY LINES OF THE PALM

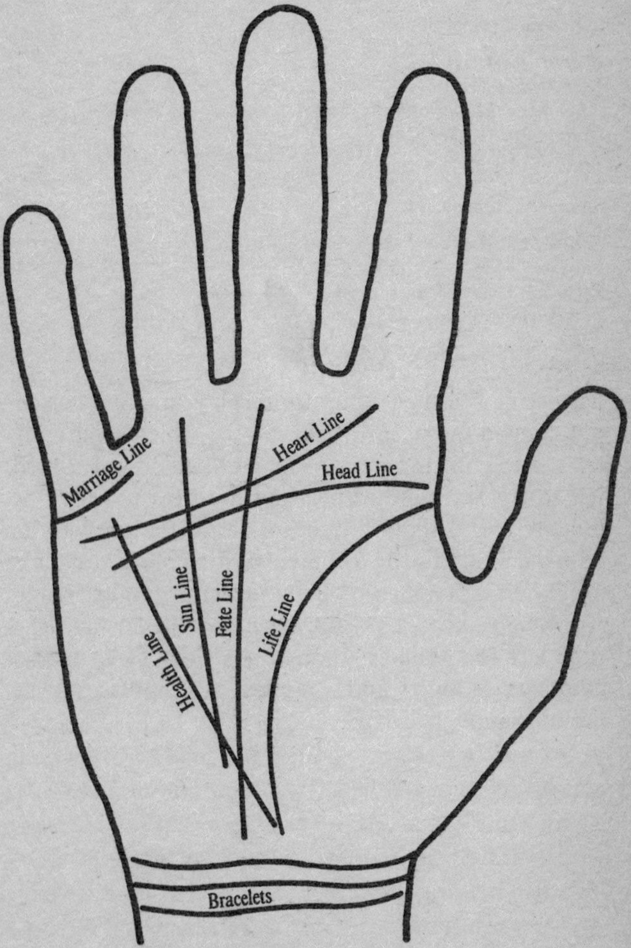

Marriage Line

Heart Line

Head Line

Health Line

Sun Line

Fate Line

Life Line

Bracelets

Chapter One

No storm or howling wolf was needed. The house that stood at the top of the hill on a street of Victorians looked as if it belonged in an Edgar Allan Poe tale. Even under bright June sunlight, the building was shrouded by the darkness of age and lengthening shadows from surrounding weeping willows.

David Logan slowed his Jeep. Though he'd been born and raised in the small Wisconsin town, he'd always been fascinated by the house. With its gables and octagonal turrets and verandas with latticelike ornamentation, it reminded him of an eerie domain suitable for any gothic tale or horror movie. Wooden steps lead to the porch and to the beveled-glass front door with its gleaming brass door knocker. On dark, stormy nights when fingers of lightning illuminated the outside of the house in a bizarre cast, an overzealous imagination could visualize a knife-wielding pyscho creeping down the stairs.

Gossipers clung to a tale that the house was haunted by the spirit of Morgana Mulvane. David had heard the story and another that several hundred years ago one of the Mulvanes had been a witch. He'd never believed the stories, but he'd always thought the present occupant, Jillian Mulvane, was bewitching enough to cast a spell over any man.

A sign in one second-floor window announced the name of her store—Stargazer. The parlor and the dining room on the first floor had been converted into the shop. It catered to the tourists who were lured to the mystical world of palmistry, numerology, and astrological readings. The summer people loved the shop with its uncanny ambience, creaky floorboards, and groaning doors. The townspeople tolerated such "nonsense" as readings by Madam Jilliana. During another time in history, David realized that he'd probably have died defending her from being burned at the stake. He wasn't a do-gooder or a believer in her hocus-pocus, but justice ranked high in his mind. Justice for everyone.

As a kid, he'd been an underdog. As an adult, he'd become a crusader for them. After all, as a lawyer, he believed that everyone deserved the best counsel. In moments of honesty, he recognized that he was still battling the ghosts that had haunted his youth. And privately, he felt like a kindred soul with the Mulvane clan who were all a touch out of pace with Lakeside. But like Jillian Mulvane's neighbors, he viewed the reading of crystal balls and tarot cards as foolish as chanting abracadabra. Spells were silly superstitions.

To his logical mind, witches and haunting spirits belonged to Halloween make-believe, not the real world.

Jillian looked up from opening a crate of books about cosmo energy. The two gray-haired women at the far end of the shop were regulars. They visited every few days to delight over any new items. Today, their interest was centered on a shipment of crystal balls that Jillian had unpacked the night before.

"That man is driving me crazy," Cornelia Quinton said in her squeaky voice. She went on, unaware that her companion, Iris Ogilvy, was more enraptured with her reflection in the crystal ball than in the love life of her friend. "But Jillian says that's natural. He's a Virgo, you see."

"Ahh," Iris responded on cue and set down the crystal ball. "Well, you shouldn't have gotten involved with him in the first place," she countered. "If he's a Virgo, you knew what you were getting. Friendship first," Iris stated knowingly.

"Yes," Cornelia said in an annoyed tone. "I know. Jillian warned me to be prepared for a long wait. But if I'm patient, he will ask me."

"But are you compatible?" Iris questioned.

"Perfectly. You know that I'm a Taurus."

Jillian smiled as the women wound a path around shelves of bottles filled with herbs, tea and potions. Each step they took toward the cash register was interrupted while one of them sniffed at a potion bottle, or examined an amulet, or peered at one of the many astrological charts adorning the walls of the deep red-purple-and-black room.

Cornelia thrust tarot cards and a package of herbal tea at Jillian. "I'll take these."

Jillian bagged them, while, as if mesmerized, Iris followed the slow circular movement of the spheres hanging from the black ceiling. "Before she married Todd, I wish my Mary Ellen had come to you for a reading, Jillian." The woman shook her head sadly. "So incompatible."

"Some couples do well even when their ascendants are in opposition," Jillian assured her.

"Oh, I hope so." Iris sighed heavily and resumed her fascination with the rotating orbs overhead. Concentrating on Saturn's rings, she lamented her daughter's woes. "Mary Ellen likes to go places. He likes to read." She paused briefly in response to the ringing telephone. "They're so different."

Jillian stretched behind her for the telephone receiver. "Stargazer, Jillian speaking."

"Jill, thank goodness."

She pressed the receiver closer to her ear to hear her brother over Iris's chatter. "Andy, you have to speak louder."

"I'm entitled to one phone call, sis. And you're it."

"What are you talking about?"

"I'm in jail," he yelled.

"You're what?"

"In jail. The sheriff's deputy arrested me."

"For what?"

"Possession of—"

His words came out jarbled as Cornelia spoke louder in deference to Iris's poor hearing.

"For what?" Jill asked again. As she caught fragments of his answer, she swayed back against the counter of shelves stocked with ginger jars. "You wouldn't," she returned. "You couldn't."

"You know that, and I know that, but they don't. Would you come down here?"

"I'll be right there." She shrugged out of her multicolored smock while setting the receiver back in its cradle. "Ladies, excuse me," she said, interrupting their disagreement about a horoscope chart by Ptolemy. "I have to close the shop for a little while."

Both women gave her their full attention.

"Do you have a problem?" Iris asked with genuine concern.

"I hope not." Jillian rounded the counter and hurried down the five steps from the loft. In a swift move, she handed Cornelia her bag while ushering both women toward the door.

At the doorway, Iris balked. Her short, round body suddenly became unmovable. "I have a reading tonight." Thoughtfully she stared at Jillian. "I feel an odd aura. I need to know if it's a happy or sad one."

"We'll find out tonight," Jillian said, grabbing her cape from a coatrack hook.

"Will you make some chamomile tea?" Iris asked, inching forward and beaming at her companion. "She makes it a special way, you know."

Jillian returned the woman's smile and scooted her out the door. "I'll have it made when you come this evening."

As the women strolled down the stairs, Jillian flicked off the switch that rotated the spheres. She was one foot out the door. Stopping, she looked back then whirled toward a nearby counter. Andy might need all the help he could get, she mused. With an amulet in her hand, she rushed outside.

David glanced back in his rearview mirror. Strolling down the middle of the road behind him was a vision from another century. He knew only one woman who wore a black hooded cape. A tall, lean woman, Jillian made him think of a bending willow. Wispy, graceful and flexible.

Without thinking, he braked then threw the shift into reverse. Jillian Mulvane lived in a whimsical, nonsensical world, one that was too far from David's for him to consider involvement with her. Still, he'd always been bowled over by this particular "crazy Mulvane." Whether she was wrong for him or not, he'd never spent a dull moment in her company. "Need a lift to town?" he yelled out the window.

Surprise registered on her face before she gave him a responding smile.

David flicked off the radio, cutting short the mellow tones of Whitney Houston. As Jillian settled on the car seat, he noted the purple peasant blouse and tan skirt beneath the cape.

"Thanks." With a hand, she brushed back strands of hair. Several bracelets dangling from her wrist echoed every movement. "I was going to take my bike, but then I remembered that I had a flat tire. I should have gotten it fixed," she went on. "It happened last Monday. It was from one of the nails that Billy Schumaker dropped on the road."

He stared at her for a long moment before shifting into drive. "You don't have a car?"

She shook her head.

"If you know that Billy did it, then his father should pay for your new tire."

She smiled wide. "Spoken like a lawyer."

David frowned, puzzled.

"He didn't throw the nails on the road. He was coming back from the hardware store with a box of nails for his dad and dropped them. I helped him pick them up, but we must have missed one, because I had a flat on my bike when I got home. I should have known."

"Known what?"

"I'm an Aquarian."

He shouldn't ask, he mused, but he couldn't seem to help himself. "What does that mean?"

"Aquarians are ruled by Uranus. That's why I should always be ready for the unexpected."

David slid a glance at her.

"And on that particular day, I was doing what Aquarians do best. Avoiding routine." She frowned at the cellophane candy wrappers balled in the Jeep ashtray and strewn in the tray between the seats. The hint of messiness seemed out of character for him. "I took a different way home than usual and was unlucky."

"Why didn't you get the tire fixed?"

"I meant to, but I had a psychic reading with Mrs. Doyles, and she was upset, so—"

"The mayor's wife?"

"Shh," she cautioned with a flashing smile. "That's a secret."

"What is?"

Jillian touched his arm. "That she comes to me for psychic readings."

"I can guess why."

"Well, anyway, Mrs. Doyles was upset, so I sat and meditated with her. Then we had some herbal tea." She settled back against the door to stare at him. His brown hair was windblown, his skin tanned from hours under the sun. He usually looked so proper, so immaculate. She eyed his blue plaid shirt, his dirty jeans, his unshaven face. The ruggedness suited him as much as his usual three-piece suit did. "Have you been fishing?"

"The scent of the lake lingers?"

She grinned and sniffed hard. "'Fraid so." When he glanced and met her eyes, she noted his were a warm, golden-brown color. "Where did you go fishing?"

"Lake Bennett."

"Away from it all?"

"I needed a few days off."

"Catch many?" she asked.

"Enough for a good dinner or two. Do you fish?"

"Everyone who lives here does."

He set his arm on the edge of the open window. "It's the first time I've gone fishing in the past two years."

"That's because you're a workaholic."

"Who says?"

"Everyone." She fiddled with the fuchsia headband holding her red hair in place. "This is nice," she commented, setting her head back and closing her eyes.

"What is?"

"Your car. I don't allow myself time to relax often during the day. But unlike a bike, a car requires little effort."

Her eyes remained closed, her lashes spiky shadows on her cheeks. He smiled. "You should get a car."

"I have no need for one."

"Everyone does."

"Not me. I wouldn't think of pumping more carbon dioxide into the air for a mile trip to town," she said in a tone that sounded amazingly practical and logical for her. "Or for when I occasionally go out to the lake on nights of a new moon."

"Why on those nights?" David swore at himself the moment that he asked the question.

She opened her eyes and bent slightly forward to peer out the window at the bright sun. "On nights when the moon is new, the moon's face is shadowed and more stars can be seen," she said distractedly.

How could such an odd conversation make sense? He wondered. "Do you make a good living at that business?"

"I enjoy it."

"I enjoy fishing, but I couldn't earn a living doing it."

"Too bad."

"What is?"

"That you don't enjoy what you do every day."

"I like law," he said quickly, then laughed at himself for feeling a need to defend it.

She returned his smile. "I know you do. And you're good. That's important, too."

"I have to be. I don't know how to hex opponents."

His dry humor made her smile. Still waters run deep, she mused. The cliché suited him. "I wouldn't do that, either."

"You don't have that power?"

She flipped down the sun visor before slanting a look at him. "Oh, I'm sure that I do. But I only believe in good charms and happy thoughts."

"So hexes are out?"

"Absolutely."

He gave her a long, solemn look. She was still wacko, he mused, and still incredibly beautiful.

She turned a quizzical expression on him. "If you came from the lake, why were you coming into town on this road? Wouldn't you make better time by traveling the other way around the lake?"

"Probably. But I like your house."

"My house?" she asked in incredulity.

"It's different."

"Spooky?"

"Sort of."

"Everyone says that," she admitted. "I love it."

"Somehow, I knew you would. Why? Because it's different?"

"Because it suits me."

"Because it's different."

"Different isn't bad," she assured him. "You ask a lot of questions."

Her candor made him smile. "I'm well trained."

"And you skirt questions. Are you afraid you'll reveal too much, counselor?"

"I suppose it can't be helped with you."

Jillian tilted her head quizzically.

"You can read my mind, can't you?"

Her eyes sparkled with some private joke. "I don't read minds."

He was relieved. For the past few moments, he kept wondering if her skin's softness was an illusion. He'd seen her walking and had wondered if he would feel the same attraction that he'd felt years ago whenever she'd been near. Now he knew nothing had changed.

She laughed suddenly and touched his hand on the steering wheel. "Carolyn Logan's big brother is as serious as ever, isn't he?"

He frowned, unsure if she was subtly complimenting or insulting him. "Is that how you see me?"

"First impressions are lasting," she answered. How often during her youth had she attempted to make friends only to have someone mock her about her mother's psychic power? How many times had some boy taunted her with a high-pitched howling sound? she reflected. But not David—his rare teasing had always been good-natured. "You used to call me Merlin's niece."

David laughed. She'd been good friends with his sister through high school. Because Carolyn had been severely shy, she'd been considered an oddball. She'd gravitated toward Jillian. "Carolyn told you that?"

"Yes."

"I didn't realize that my sister talked about me so much."

"I always asked about you," she admitted easily. "I had an enormous crush on you."

"Did you?"

She heard the surprise in his voice and smiled. "I thought older men were enigmatic."

"Older?" He grimaced. "I haven't even got a gray hair."

"At fourteen, I viewed seventeen as incredibly old."

David kept his eyes on the road. "And now?" he asked.

"And now, I'm a month away from thirty. That seems like a wonderful age, a young age," she added. "A coming-alive age. Old enough to have made a few mistakes and gained some wisdom. And young enough to make a few more mistakes without feeling as if I should know better."

But he did know better, he cautioned himself. He rarely got involved in anything that he didn't feel he could grasp some control over. And no one would ever control this woman. Years ago, as if making a statement, she'd set herself apart from the crowd with her eccentric clothes and manner.

Good sense had warned him to keep his distance. He'd worked hard to make the name Logan respectable. Wasn't that why he'd returned to Lakeside after law school? Wasn't that why he'd always wanted to hang his shingle in the town where he'd been born? He'd felt almost compelled to do so. If honest, he'd admit that he'd been driven to prove something to everyone who'd ever made a snide remark about any Logan. He'd wanted to walk among the people who'd looked down their noses at him all those years. No one did now. He lived on Dover Circle next door to Agnes Simpson and Lakeside's mayor, Herbert Doyles. He was invited to their dinner parties. He was the one they consulted when they needed legal advice. He'd accomplished goals that he'd set for himself when he'd been twelve years old. He'd firmly walked the line of respectability.

"Stop at the sheriff's office, please."

She was suddenly silent beside him, staring thoughtfully, too thoughtfully at him.

"Andy is in jail," she said with an abruptness that made her voice sound strained.

David frowned at her. "Your brother's been arrested?"

"Yes." She looked slightly stunned as if only good fortune was supposed to fall on her family. "You know Andy. He's not the kind to be dishonest."

"People don't always live up to our expectations."

"Andy is innocent. He's my brother. I know that he's innocent. Wouldn't you believe in your younger brother?"

David had lost blind faith in a loved one years ago. "Not always," he answered as he concentrated on looking for a parking space outside the sheriff's office.

She dug into her purse. "I do. But for good measure, I have this for him."

David braked then eyed the acorn in her hand. "What is that?"

"An amulet."

"An acorn on a chain?"

"If you carry an acorn, you'll have good luck and a long life."

"Are you giving that to Andy?"

She nodded. "He needs extra good luck now."

"You don't really believe—"

She arched a brow, stopping him. Leaning toward the ignition, with a slender finger she flicked the rabbit's foot hanging on his key ring. "Everyone looks for something to help bring them good luck."

"He might need more than good wishes."

"He might." She stared speculatively at him. "But any lawyer who defends a Mulvane is prime for criticism."

David said nothing. Several of the town's more upstanding citizens followed Agnes Simpson's lead about everything. Agnes had never been shy about voicing her dislike for the Mulvanes. She claimed that fortune-tellers presented the wrong image of Lakeside. David assumed since Andy was a relative of Jillian's, Agnes's same snooty attitude applied to him.

Jillian pushed open the car door. "Thanks for the ride."

She offered her hand to him as a test. Though she capitalized on an airhead image to promote her store, she wasn't obtuse to her own feelings. Palpitations of the heart had nothing to do with health when an almost-thirty-year-old woman was talking to an attractive man. And she never ignored a warning.

"Anytime," he answered, feeling reluctant to release her hand.

She saw something flicker in his eyes. Years ago, as a teenager, her toes would have curled from it. Today, as a woman, she'd thought that she would be immune to him.

She was wrong.

He watched her leave. He'd like to see her again. And her brother needed more than an amulet. He needed a lawyer.

As she reached the door of the sheriff's office, she paused abruptly as if ill then slowly looked back over her shoulder at him. She gave him a half smile as if she'd just learned something that he had no knowledge of. Mysterious, he mused again. Intriguing. Dangerous to him, David decided and shifted the gear into drive.

Chapter Two

The scent of leather and wood greeted David as he walked into his office. The familiar sight of his massive oak desk in the adjoining room stirred an anxiousness to get back to work. He'd needed time off. He'd driven himself for the past year on several cases and loved every moment of it, but he'd felt fatigued. Spending a week alone camping and fishing had recharged his desire for work.

Myra Hopkins swiveled her chair away from the bay window and toward her desk. "Will the real David Logan stand up," she quipped.

He scratched the whiskers shadowing his jaw. "What do you think? Would the good citizens of Lakeside accept a lawyer with a beard?"

Myra squinted at him. "All the females under forty would."

"That's no compliment. In a town this size, any male who's single and breathing is fair game."

"Why are you back so soon?"

"I told you that I'd be gone only a week."

"I'd hoped that you'd give yourself a little more time."

He grinned at her. "Mother hens went out of style a decade ago."

"Nagging didn't."

Friends with his mother years ago, Myra had marched into his office before his shingle had been hung and had announced that he needed a secretary who cared. David had never regretted hiring her.

"I saw you drive up." She smiled knowingly. "I love this bay window. That's why I came to work here."

"The perfect vantage point for a nosy woman?"

Her chin lifted slightly. "Not nosy. Inquisitive."

"Same thing."

"You were with Jillian Mulvane," she added, ignoring his previous comment.

"I gave her a ride into town."

Myra nodded, attempting a blasé expression.

"Nothing more," David said a bit defensively.

"Wouldn't have expected differently."

He frowned. "Why?"

"Because she isn't the kind of woman for Lakeside's most prominent lawyer, is she?" Her head bent, she busily stacked notes as if no response was necessary from him.

David noted that she'd bought a new shade of nail polish. She was a neat woman with curly, grayish-brown hair brushed away from her face. When unsmiling, she looked unapproachable and stern, the lines from fifty-some years deeply etched in her face. She usually wore simple dark skirts and white blouses, and a cameo broach, a gift from her late husband. But behind that staid demeanor lurked a flair for flamboyance. This morning's nail polish was a bright coral.

At his quietness, she looked up. "About your passenger, she's—"

"She's still the same." *Beautiful,* he mused. *And wacko.*

"The same?"

David focused on her. "I haven't talked to Jillian in years. She's the same, still involved in hocus-pocus."

Myra gave him an indulgent smile. "Why haven't you talked to her before this?"

"I didn't mean that. We've said hello."

"Hello, isn't talking to someone. It's a greeting." Her elbows on her desk, she pushed her glasses forward and peered at him. "You should talk to her more. She's one of the most interesting people in this town."

"Yes."

"Intriguing."

"Yes," David answered absently. She intrigued him with her smile. It was quick and disarming. It made him feel as if he could tell her a deep, dark secret, and she'd not only listen but also care.

"Attractive."

David snapped himself back to his surroundings. "Definitely. But she doesn't have a foot on the ground."

"I suppose that's the impression she gives."

He moved closer to her desk. "Myra, she plays with tarot cards."

"She doesn't play with them. She foresees the future with them."

"Are you listening to yourself? I know that you have more sense, more intelligence—"

"Glad you realized that," Myra interrupted with a smile.

David matched her grin.

"She's not as flaky as she seems," she added.

"Did she cast a spell on you?"

"Now you're talking crazy. She's not a witch."

"So you don't believe in her mumbo jumbo?"

"I knew her mother, David. We were good friends."

He perched on the edge of her desk. "Were you? When?"

"Through school. And later."

"What was she like?"

"Different." She smiled reflectively. "She used to brighten my day."

He looked out the window toward the sheriff's office. Funny, he'd have said the same thing about her daughter.

"She claimed to have visions."

"Visions?" Jamming a hand into the pocket of his jeans, David waited while she pushed her glasses up from the bridge of her nose.

"The gossipers are to blame for how people viewed the Mulvanes. Everyone always called them the loony Mulvanes."

"And you disagree?" he asked though he knew the answer.

"I'm my own person, thank you." A serious look settled on her face. "Jillian isn't loony."

David rocked a hand in a maybe gesture. "The mother was kind of crazy."

"Says who?"

"Says Agnes."

"You know what I think about Agnes Simpson. She's a bitter old woman."

"I know that her tongue has a biting edge but—"

"No, buts," she countered, "Jillian is normal. She just emphasizes her eccentricities. That's all. Charms people with them."

"Charming or not, she should be using more common sense about Andy. He needs—"

"A lawyer."

David narrowed an eye at her but said nothing.

"I feel so sorry for Andy. He works hard. He doesn't deserve this kind of trouble. The sheriff arrested him a little while ago."

"Did you see that from your lookout window?"

She made a face. "Never mind. We're not discussing me. We're talking about him. And he might need a lawyer."

David turned silent again.

"And she might want to hire the best in town," she added, pointing a finger at him.

"Flattery helps you keep this job."

"I know," she bantered. "You have some messages." She held out sheets of paper. "One is from Matt."

David reached for the note.

"He's coming home for a visit," she informed him before releasing the paper to him.

David frowned instinctively. "I wonder why he's coming home."

"It's summertime."

David shook his head. "No, he usually works near campus for extra money during the summer."

"You're worrying about nothing."

"My kid brother drives me crazy."

"You used to worry about your sister, Carolyn, too, didn't you?"

"Didn't I," he said rather than asked. "She was good friends with Jillian. Carolyn and I used to have some knockout arguments about that."

"Her friendship with Jillian?"

"No, not exactly that. But Carolyn was awfully impressionable. I kept worrying that Jillian would talk her into going to Alaska and opening up a business to sell whale oil or something crazy like that."

"See, you worried for nothing. Carolyn leads a nice respectable life. She's a registered nurse, married, with two kids. Normal. I would think because of your sister's close friendship with Jillian, you'd feel some obligation to help the Mulvanes."

He sorted through the messages. "You never give up, do you?"

"It's my suppressed motherly instincts. If my daughter and her family lived closer, then you'd see less of my endearing qualities." She touched his hand, stopping him. "Forget them. This is the one that counts." She waved a note marked Urgent at him. "Agnes called. She's ready to lay an egg."

He clucked his tone. "Vicious lady."

"Who? Her?"

"You," he teased. "Anything else to tell me?"

"Everything else is absolutely groovy these days."

He shook his head. "That granddaughter of yours is a bad influence." He pushed away from the desk and turned toward his office. "I'll let you know how groovy everything really is in a few minutes."

"Going to call Agnes, huh?"

"Right," he said, heading into his office.

"The acorn has always been a good-luck symbol, Andy."

He nodded but continued to frown.

Jillian worried about him. Though only two years younger than she, he looked like an uncertain teenager at the moment. His light brown hair was mussed, his jaw unshaven, his eyes dull. He looked scared.

"I don't know what I'm going to do, Jill."

"You'll be fine," she assured him, placing a hand on his arm. "Tell me everything."

"I have."

"Everything you can remember about that man—what's his name?"

"Siverson. But what's the use?" he said, sounding downtrodden.

"Andy, don't do that. Mulvanes never give up. Do we?"

He raised his face and stared for a long moment at her. Jillian kept her smile firm for his sake.

"No." He nodded his head as if prodding himself. "No, we don't."

"And we don't look back. Didn't Mama teach us to look only toward the future?"

"Yeah." His soft brown eyes smiled. "But for my peace of mind, could you tell me something?"

"What?"

"How does my future look?"

Her hand slid down to his and clasped it. "I don't see you eating bread and water in a jail cell."

As he laughed low, Jillian relaxed. If his spirits stayed up, they'd win. "You know that half of a person's problems in life exist because they give up before tackling them. If they'd just set out to beat them, then the problems would be gone before they begin."

His smile widened. "I'm glad that you came."

"Tomorrow, you'll be out of here," she said with a conviction she didn't really feel at the moment.

"That depends on the bail that's set at the court hearing."

"I'll raise the bail." She squeezed his hand. "I'll be back later with your suit. But first, I have to talk to someone."

"Who?" he asked, standing with her.

"Andy, we can't win unless we help ourselves."

He frowned in puzzlement at her.

"I'm going to get you the best lawyer in town."

"We can't afford him."

"Yes, we can," she insisted.

"He won't take my case."

"He will," Jillian said with feigned certainty.

"He won't understand how I could get into this mess."

Probably not, Jillian mused.

"David Logan reminds me of Fred," he said.

Jillian met his eyes. "How do you remember Fred?"

"I was eight when Mama was still married to him."

Jillian shook her head. "He reminds me more of Lawrence."

"Number three?"

"No, he was Mama's fourth," she reminded him. "Remember. He was the handsome one."

"And such a—" He rolled his eyes. "He was such a stickler for everything being right."

"Proper." Jillian watched Andy toying with the amulet. "That's David Logan."

"Number four was the wrong kind for Mama."

"Uh huh. So were one, two and three."

"Jill?"

She looked up.

Andy's brows knitted with concern. "You aren't—well—you'll stay away from him, won't you?"

Jillian didn't need a reminder to keep her distance from David. She'd been reminding herself of the same thing ever since she'd left his car. At certain times his manner resembled another man's, one who'd taught her a lesson in caution. So trustingly, she'd reached out to Jason Langley expecting unconditional love. She knew now it didn't exist. "Andy, don't be worrying about me. You're the one who needs David Logan's help."

"He won't take my case."

"He will."

"You're sure?" he asked.

"It's in the cards."

"She wasn't home," David said as he stepped out of his office.

Standing in front of the bay window, Myra looked over her shoulder at him. "Agnes?"

"Her maid rambled about what time Agnes had left, what time she'd be back, would I call then, and a half dozen other questions. She sounded as if she was sending out an SOS."

"Agnes must be on the warpath then," Myra deducted. "That's not news. She's always crotchety. Never have I known a woman who had such a bitter taste in her mouth all the time. Last month she was complaining about the Boy Scouts selling candy bars in front of the grocery store."

"That makes sense if you remember that she's one of the owners of the grocery store."

"She could be a little charitable since she owns most of this town."

"You'd never convince her of that."

"You'll get your saint's wings for all the work you do for her."

"She pays me well, Myra."

"Is that why you put up with her orneriness?"

"A little honey goes a long way."

"You need a bucket of it to sweeten that woman. And that snooty Lillian Hilden isn't much better. No wonder they're such buddies. Without the luck of matrimony, neither of them would be so high-and-mighty now. If Hugh Simpson hadn't married Agnes Fursam, then she'd have gone after his older brother, William, eventually or someone else who'd keep her in a life-style that she claimed she was 'accustomed to.'" She gave him a disgruntled, "Humph. Her daddy was a cow farmer, nothing more."

David cocked a brow. "Fursam Dairies was more than a cow farm."

"It's all in the way you look at it."

Myra's gift for gab and gossip had, on occasion, slipped some information to him that had been useful. But when she took off on a tirade about Agnes, her tune was always the same.

"Did her maid give you an inkling of what's upsetting her?"

David shook his head and glanced down at his clothes. The aroma of fish and a camp fire clung to him. "No, but I'm going home to clean up before I go over to see her." He held back a grin. "Don't you know what the ruckus is about?"

"All I know is gossip. And you know, I've been told by my boss to stop spreading rumors."

"When did you turn over a new leaf?" he teased.

Myra snorted and walked away from her desk to resume gazing out the bay window. "Well, I'll be." With a glance back at him, she gestured with her head. "Jillian is coming this way. If she asks, will you—"

David swung away from her as the outer office door opened.

"Jillian, how nice to see you!" Myra said brightly, facing forward.

"Hi, Myra."

David watched her face brighten for Myra, but concern clouded her eyes.

"Do you have time to talk, David?"

"Talk?"

"To a client?" Jillian asked.

He hadn't considered what he would do if she wanted him to represent Andy. "Come on in," he said, pushing his office door open for her. He never had a choice, he realized. He stared into her blue eyes and knew that he'd never turn her down.

* * *

His office was exactly as Jillian had expected. Brass, leather and wood. Opposite a wall of framed degrees was a painting of a hunting dog. "You had a dog like that, didn't you?" she asked, gesturing toward the painting of the golden retriever.

"A stray."

"Carolyn told me that he was injured when you found him. Later, after he was healthy again, someone offered you a great deal of money for him, but you wouldn't sell him."

"By the looks of him when I found him, he seemed to have gone through enough. Have a seat here," he suggested, pointing toward the padded chair near his desk.

"I just came from talking to Andy at the jail." While he rounded his desk and settled behind it, she scanned the rest of the office. An abstract painting that resembled a sensuous, rainbow-colored river hung on the white wall adjacent to his desk. It was the one touch of bright color in the sober, respectable-looking room with its forest green carpet, leather chairs and settee. "Obviously he needs a lawyer." Her head bent, she tightened her fingers around the straps of her shoulder bag. "At first, I didn't think that they could hold him."

"Why did you think that?"

She met his eyes. "Circumstantial evidence."

"It must be more than circumstantial. What's he been arrested for?"

"Possession of stolen auto parts, which is ridiculous. Andy doesn't steal."

David pushed his wing chair away from the desk. "What happened with the sheriff?"

"Andy has receipts for the parts that he was selling in his auto-parts store."

"Letterhead receipts?"

"No. Just handwritten ones. The sheriff claimed that Andy could have made up phony ones to protect himself from prosecution if caught."

David leaned back in his chair. "Why doesn't he believe that the receipts are legitimate?"

"Because no one else has ever seen the man that Andy bought the parts from."

"Who is this man?"

"Earl Siverson is the name that he gave Andy. But the sheriff checked with Milwaukee and Madison criminal records. No one by that name exists. There's no police record, driver's license or FBI file on him."

"How did he approach Andy?"

She stared at the law books lined up on a shelf. He was neat and organized. She never was. "He claimed that he purchased parts in bulk, then does the travel-ing salesman routine. He must go to small shops be-cause the larger automotive shops have their own distributor." She drew a hard breath. "Will you please help?" she asked in a polite tone that was inbred in her by a mother who'd vacillated between playing Miss Manners, Auntie Mame, and the medium for W.B. Yeats. "If you don't help, I don't know who to go to."

As she shook her head, her hair fell across her cheek like glistening red threads. David wondered if it would feel as soft as it looked.

"You know us," she said, watching him balance a chess piece paperweight on his palm as if judging its weight. "Another lawyer would be influenced by—by..." She paused, annoyed that eccentricities were viewed so narrow-mindedly. "Our background doesn't exactly parallel that of the pillars of the community," she added. "Everyone remembers Grandpa Mulvane walking around town with his dowser stick looking for water. And then there was Mama. And I'm considered—"

Unsettling, David mused as she released a quiet laugh. It aroused a distinct tightening within him. He stared at the black cape with its bright red lining that she'd draped over the chair. If he took the case and spent time with her, he sensed the inevitable. Sooner or later, he'd want to make love to her. "Unique," David said softly.

Jillian met his eyes and felt her nerves flutter. "What a lovely way of putting it. But not dealing with a full deck is the usual description."

"People exaggerate."

"Thank you, but you see, I do have a problem," she reminded him. "Are you going to take the case? I know your fee is probably steep but—"

"Not too," he answered. "I haven't always lived on Dover Circle," he said. He'd come from a different beginning, one he'd never forgotten. He'd also never forgotten some of his neighbors. The ones who were loyal to his mother after his father had left them. "One client's been paying me every few weeks for two years."

"I'm not sure that I'd even manage that."

"I'm sure you couldn't. You don't have chickens."

"Chick—"

"Chickens," he repeated, smiling. "He gives me fresh eggs as payment."

Jillian smiled. "You've also received much heftier fees than that. Agnes Simpson is one of your clients, isn't she?"

"Yes."

"Will she object to your representing a Mulvane?"

"It's not her business."

Jillian studied him for a long moment. "That's brave. She usually makes everything her business."

"But she doesn't worry you, does she?" he guessed.

"No. I'm lucky that way."

"Do you really believe luck plays that big of a part in our lives? You took Andy an amulet, yet you still came here," he reminded her.

She straightened her back. "You're going to take the case, aren't you?"

David sensed a trap. "Yes, I am."

"Then the amulet did bring good luck, didn't it?"

Amusement slipped over him quickly. Nothing she said surprised him. Yet everything she said surprised him.

"I know that Andy didn't do anything wrong, so he'll be all right."

As much as David liked to believe in the justice system, he was too realistic not to be aware that judicial mistakes occurred. "Were the stolen parts in clear view, on display in Andy's store?"

"Yes, most of them. Some were still in the stockroom, but— Oh, I see what you're saying." She smiled. This time, it was filled with its usual warmth. "If they were stolen, if he *knew* they were stolen, then he wouldn't display them."

"Unlikely."

"That's good isn't it?"

"For me."

"Why?" she asked.

"It helps me believe in him. But jurors aren't quite so accepting. We need to find Siverson or someone he sold parts to. I'll check with the sheriff. When he arrested him—"

"He didn't."

He glanced down at his notepad. "Who did?"

"His deputy. Riley Fursam."

David frowned at the thought of dealing with Agnes's cousin. Childhood memories never forgotten included the obnoxious deputy. "I'll talk to Andy before his court date and—" He cut his words short as he watched her brows pinch together.

"His arraignment is tomorrow."

"Tomorrow?" David released a long breath. How had he gotten himself into this? "That won't give us much time."

"He hates it in jail. Being confined."

David imagined that was a Mulvane trait.

"Can we get him out?"

"We can try."

"About the bail—"

"Don't worry about it. I know a good bondsman."

Tension eased from her. She realized that she was clinging to his logic and sensibility. "I suppose that it sounds dumb to you that Andy would purchase the parts without checking out the distributor."

"No. A lot of people purchase in good faith. Did the man ever give him a purchase order or a business card, or anything like that?"

"Just the handwritten receipts."

"What if Andy wanted to buy more parts from him? How did he contact him?"

"He had the man's phone number. Andy gave that information to the sheriff right away so he could check out his story."

"Did the sheriff investigate?"

Jillian frowned. "Yes."

"What aren't you saying?" he asked softly.

She felt a tinge of annoyance sweep through her. It was a silly response. David wasn't responsible for the problem, but he was bringing it to the forefront. She fought worry. "The phone number belonged to a pizza parlor."

David heard her, but his mind had shifted to the prosecutor's case. He shoved his chair back from his desk and pushed himself to a stand.

"Andy isn't lying," she insisted.

He saw agitation in her eyes. She has a passionate nature, he thought. She'd argue in Andy's defense until her voice gave out. "Take it easy." He rested a hip on the edge of the desk and touched her shoulder. Instantly he knew that he'd been wrong in moving closer. Her flowery scent drifted up to him.

Like a warning, sensation skittered up her spine. His intellect, his careful nature, his propensity for details were valuable qualities, necessary to help Andy. But she and David would never understand each other. He was quiet and reserved, pragmatic. She was an idealist. They were opposites. Yet, despite all those reminders, the firm, comforting hand on her shoulder made her wonder if his caress would be gentle or demanding. Jillian gave her head a shake. Something definitely was wrong with her today. "I have to leave." In a quick, unhesitating stride, she hurried toward the door before he could protest. "I'll see you tomorrow in court," she said, looking back.

Without forethought, David had followed as if drawn by her scent. "I'll walk you out."

Surprised, she looked over her shoulder at him. "You don't have to."

He gave her a wry amused look. "I have to go home," he said with a glance down at his clothes. "This isn't exactly the perfect attire for the law office, but I came right into town to see if I had any messages. Myra?" His secretary was bent forward at the window, rubbernecking to see down the sidewalk. "Myra?"

She jumped, straightened and wheeled around to face them. "I dropped something and—"

David smiled. "Don't break your neck trying to find it."

She scowled at him.

"I'm leaving. I have to go home and change. Set up a file for Andy Mulvane."

"What about Agnes?" she asked with a smirk that she didn't even try to hide.

"I'll see her later."

Jillian stepped outside ahead of him. "When will you see Andy?"

"Now." He cupped a hand around her arm. He wasn't prone to touching any woman so easily. As with everything in his life, with women, he'd weighed the consequences of his actions. Love affairs weren't entered into or ended without consideration. He wasn't a man of impulse. Yet he'd reached for her as if it were the natural thing to do, as if compelled to touch her. "I'll contact you after I talk to him."

"At my shop?" She tipped back her head and saw his hesitation. In Lakeside, he wasn't just anyone, and neither was she. "Do you really want people to think that you're patronizing the Stargazer?"

David nearly smiled at her bluntness. "Do you think I'd care?"

She met his stare with a challenging one. "Yes, I do," she said honestly. "I think you care very much about their opinions."

David cursed himself. All his life, he'd struggled because he had cared what other people thought about him, about any Logan. He saw an expectation in her eyes. She expected him to back away. He noted a flicker of disappointment settling over her face, as if he'd already said no to meeting at her shop. Suddenly not seeing that expression seemed more important than anything else. "I'll be there. Later," he added before the impulsiveness controlling his answer registered in his mind.

Chapter Three

Later, David had said. He wouldn't come, Jillian decided. He'd never come near the Stargazer. He'd worked too hard for his respected reputation to take the chance of being seen wandering into her world of mystical fantasy.

Just as well, she decided, yanking open a desk drawer. David was the epitome of respectability and exactly the kind of man she'd vowed to stay clear of. He was too much like every man who'd charmed her mother.

She lifted out a stack of receipts from the previous day's sales. Intent on tallying them, she didn't hear the sound of car tires crunching on the gravel in the driveway, she wasn't prepared for the heaviness that suddenly pressed against her chest.

As if the sunshine pouring into the room from the domed sun window had been eclipsed by a thick, foreboding cloud, the room seemed to darken. A familiar sense of dread swept through her. Dismal, depressing, it weighed down on her like a heavy curtain that made even breathing seem difficult.

With a shiver, she crossed her arms over her chest protectively and fought the sensation and the inevitable vision. Her eyes squeezed tight, she battled the all-too-familiar warning sign of trouble.

A spinning wagon wheel flashed before her. She shook her head to banish more images. Almost excruciatingly slow, the heaviness and the soundless vacuum rescinded. Only then did she relax back against the chair. Months had passed since she'd had a vision. Why now? Why had she allowed herself to drop her guard? Feeling drained, she drew several deep breaths, but the only outward sign of her past struggle was the perspiration bathing the back of her neck. These moments were hers alone. No one could share in them. No one could understand them. For a few seconds, she stood alone in a world that was neither reality nor fantasy. And she was completely alone, Jillian mused, placing her hand to her warm face. That was what she'd always hated most about the visions. But she had little choice. She'd seen her mother ridiculed and had promised herself that she'd keep her own clairvoyance a secret.

"Jillian?"

She jumped at the male voice and swiveled her head toward the shop doorway. Her usual greeting smile wouldn't form. She stared at Riley Fursam's bulky form, at his deputy's badge and knew her premonition was on target. Trouble had just walked into her shop.

As if he had no resistance, David couldn't stop thinking about her. Her scent had haunted him when he'd passed his neighbor's lilac bush. Her smile had lingered in his mind as he'd opened the house and let sunshine into the rooms. An image of her hair with its fiery red sheen had flashed before him when he'd turned on the flame beneath the coffeepot.

Showered and shaved, David tugged on clean jeans and then pulled a shirt over his head. He was allowing ordinary masculine responses to an extremely feminine and beautiful woman to confuse him. What else would account for his daydreaming about her? he wondered, searching for a logical explanation.

He had one shoe on when the phone rang. With his other shoe dangling from his fingers, he raced into the kitchen and snatched up the telephone receiver. "Hello."

"Dave?" The male voice was young and eager yet threaded with uncertainty.

"Matt, hi," David said with a forced brightness as he warily waited for the reason behind his younger brother's phone call.

While Matt offered a quick rundown of his past two months at college in a breezy three-minute monologue, David hunted for something to eat. The aroma of percolated coffee drifted back to him as he poured a cup. "When will you be home?" David finally asked.

"In a couple of days. We need to talk."

David leaned a jean-clad hip against the kitchen counter and dunked a stale doughnut in his coffee cup. "If it's about your leaving school, I don't want to talk."

"Dave, it's my life. I can do what I want. I'm only talking to you about this because you—hell, you worked hard to help all of us get an education, but—" He paused and then appealed, "I'm different from you."

"The free spirit," David mumbled in a tone more caustic than he intended.

"You've always known what you wanted, so you never wanted to search for anything else," Matt said in a hesitant manner as if groping for the right, convincing words.

David washed down a bite of the doughnut and rubbed his powder-sugar-covered fingers over a dish towel. "We'll talk when you get here."

"Dave, I'm not—"

"We'll talk then."

Under his breath, Matt grumbled an earthy comment.

David couldn't help smiling at his brother's predictable response to frustration. "Hey."

"Yeah?" his brother responded in a surly tone.

"It'll be good to see you."

A trace of a smile edged Matt's voice again. "Ditto."

David tossed the rest of his doughnut in the garbage pail. Did his brother really think that the same carefree thoughts had never passed through his mind? How often had he wanted to chuck it all, run off with some beautiful, smiling woman, someone like Jillian who viewed the world with a less pragmatic eye, who said outrageous things that sounded oddly intelligent to him? The woman rambled nonstop one moment then fell into thoughtful, pensive moods so quickly that she baffled him. Fascinated him. She was light and sunshine and warmth. He smiled. She was dark and exotic and mysterious. She was a beautiful kook, he thought, glancing at the telephone. He'd set high standards for himself and for his brother and sister. He'd had to. His father had forced them to live irreproachable lives, to prove that not every Logan was as unscrupulous as he'd been.

Matt had been too young to remember the months of shame that David and his mother had endured. If he had, he might understand why David held such a tight rein on his life. And Jillian could complicate it, he admitted honestly to himself. She wasn't his type. He downed his coffee and swung away from the counter. Balancing on one leg, he slipped on his other shoe. He wouldn't think about her anymore. He wouldn't call her. He didn't need to hear her voice. Even as he completed the thought, he headed toward the back door. No, he didn't need to hear her voice, but he definitely wanted to see her again.

Few things left Jillian speechless. But as she listened to Deputy Riley Fursam, she felt numb. No one could have this kind of day, she mused.

"It's the third complaint, so you'll have to—"

The bell above the door tinkled again, interrupting him. Jillian tensed. She didn't need a customer hearing Riley's condemnations. She prayed the next person who entered her shop wasn't Iris's sister, Muriel.

The woman could spread gossip from one end of town to the other in less than two hours.

Jillian had never believed in chivalrous knights on white horses or macho Rambo types. But looking past Riley, she wondered if she had her own personal Superman. "David, how nice," she gushed and scooted around Riley's bulk. Stopping inches from David, she gave him a thank-you smile. "I'm glad you came."

Unsure why he'd received it, David returned a reluctant one before glancing at Riley. "Is he here about Andy?" he asked low.

Jillian shook her head. "No. I can't believe anyone's day can go like this," she said through barely moving lips.

Riley stopped beside them in the doorway. "I'll be leaving. But don't forget what I've told you."

David frowned at the tone he'd used. Even when Riley wasn't in uniform, he annoyed David. And the sight of the barrel-stomached man standing toe-to-toe with this delicate, red-haired woman raised an ire David hadn't felt since his youth. Taking one step to the side, he placed himself between Jillian and the deputy. "You said that you were leaving, didn't you?"

Riley's eyes met his. "I wouldn't get involved in any of this if I were you, Logan."

"It's nice of you to look out for my best interests, but I still don't follow the leader well."

"Too bad." Riley's mouth twisted in a wry smirk. "Guess you're slow at learning your lessons then."

Jillian waited until the door closed behind him. "Not smart, David."

"What isn't?"

"Siding with a Mulvane."

As if he hadn't heard her, he eyed the room with interest. "I thought magic was powerful."

Jillian turned away on a laugh. "Very powerful. But I don't know how to turn him into a toad."

"Too bad. How about a weasel?"

She looked back with a smile. His dark head bent, he was scanning shelves of books.

"He and I go back a long way," David explained, frowning at the book titles. One was about terrestrial astrology. Whatever that was, David mused. Another book's title was about the teachings of Geomancy. Despite years of education, he felt suddenly uninformed. She lived in a world totally alien from his. "Riley's always liked bullying."

"You?"

He heard amazement in her voice and smiled. "At twelve, I was more vulnerable. He'd strut around town with the knowledge that a cousin of the Simpsons could do whatever he wanted. He's never outgrown the childish need to intimidate people."

She shrugged as if Riley didn't matter.

"And he's still choosing smaller opponents," David added.

Jillian reassured him. "I guess I could work on the weasel curse."

David laughed and then swept out his arm. Decorated in mostly black and varying shades of red and purple, the shop should have seemed dark and depressing, but the skylight and the long, narrow windows along the walls filled the room with light. "How did you get started in this?"

"By this, I guess, you mean fortune-telling?"

He nodded.

"Haven't you heard? My mother comes from a family of eccentrics."

"Be serious."

"I am. I told you Grandpa Mulvane was a dowser. He used to help farmers search for water before they drilled for their wells."

He turned over a statue of a nude holding a hunting horn. At her feet was a crab. "Was he successful?"

"Very. That represents Luna. The crab is the astrological symbol of Cancer."

He touched the tip of the hunting horn and stared expectantly at her, waiting for an answer.

"She's identified with Diana, the Roman goddess of the moon."

She could have been talking in a foreign language to him, David decided, giving her a nod in response.

Steadily he moved from one display counter to the next. She hadn't expected him to show such genuine interest in everything. She hadn't anticipated the tense undercurrent that charged between them whenever their eyes met.

"Do you have any help here?"

"Occasionally during the summer, a college girl helps out."

"Where is she?"

"She decided to take a trip this year. She's visiting Stonehenge. No one knows if the Druids built it or if Merlin came from Ireland with the stones."

Lounging back against the counter, he followed her movements. Fluid strides. Long legs. He liked the easy way she carried herself.

Aware of his stare, she pushed her hair back while she drew a deep, calming breath. Definite vibrations were resounding in the quiet air. If she had a second to herself, she could think clearly. But as his gaze remained on her, she couldn't seem to keep any thought in her head for more than a second.

"You were talking about Merlin," David reminded her.

She planted her feet to the spot while she struggled for a tone that wouldn't reveal how unsettled she was. "One theory is that the monument was an ancient observatory. The stones are positioned in an alignment with the planets and the sun and the moon. I thought Carolyn might become an astronomer," she added. "She used to love sitting in the top window of this old house with that telescope you bought her in Madison."

"She became a nurse," he said.

"I know. A sensible job," she said in a tone that was edged with disappointment.

Curiosity got the best of him. "I thought so," he answered distractedly while strolling up the steps toward the loft. On the top step, he stopped. He caught himself gaping and snapped his mouth tight.

The high ceiling in the loft was painted black. Sparkling Italian lights winked like stars. Giant spheres on wires floated in slow circles around the ceiling like planetary orbs in the universe. Hanging from overhead rafters in an alcove at the back of the shop were dried weeds. A black cat was sprawled as if comatose on one glass counter and basked in the ray of sun streaming in from an octagon window.

Jillian curled a hand around the newel cap of the banister and stared up at him. "I see disbelief."

"You wouldn't need any mystic powers to do that."

"I suppose not. You don't believe in any of this, do you?"

He strolled around the loft, not answering.

"Most people say they don't believe in fortune-telling. But oddly many of those same people are anxious to have their fortunes told."

"Intellectually skeptical?" he asked with a glance down at her.

"Yes. But some people who claim they don't believe in ghosts are actually afraid of them."

David eyed the Ouija boards and boxes of dominoes. "You sell games here, too?"

"Dominoes can be used as a mode of divination."

He descended the steps. At the bottom, he paused beside a display of crystal balls. The woman lived on a different planet.

"What do you see?"

"Glossy clear rock." He looked over his shoulder at her. "What should I see?"

"The large ones are commercial ones. Real crystal balls are polished rock crystal or clear quartz. Expensive. Crystal gazing requires staring at the crystal until one enters 'inner space'," she explained.

He'd get a grip on this yet. Maybe. "Can anyone do this?"

"Few people have the inborn talent."

Though he was too polite to scoff, a scowl settled on his face.

"This has nothing to do with the occult or supernatural," she assured him. "The person disassociates his consciousness. That's not an easy thing to do. Even when you're sitting in a quiet room, you're conscious of noises. The faintest sound seems like an annoyingly loud one."

"Can you?" He turned his head toward her. "Disassociate?"

She ignored his frown and his skepticism. "My mother could. In a way," she corrected.

He noted that she'd avoided his question about her.

"She could see clouds in the crystal."

"And clouds tell the future?"

"White clouds mean good luck. Red clouds can mean disaster. It's a rather vague method."

"Why sell crystal balls then?"

"The college students love to use them in their dorm rooms for decorations. I have a good mail-order business. You'd approve," she added. "It's quite successful."

A frown etched a deep line between his brows as he strolled along a wall of shelves. "What are these?"

"Herbs and natural foods." She gestured toward a shelf. "Beans, soybeans, legumes. All of them lower the blood pressure."

"Tabasco sauce?" he asked, pointing at a bottle.

"Hot foods help protect your lungs."

"What does good health have to do with what you do?" he asked, even while telling himself that he shouldn't care about this woman's strange life-style.

"What's the point in wondering about a future if you aren't going to take good care of yourself?"

He grinned because she sounded so certain, so convinced that what she believed in was sensible. Oddly he'd found himself beginning to see some logic in what she was saying. "Your specialty is palmistry?"

"Also called chiromancy. It's been practiced since before the Middle Ages as the most popular fortune-telling method. By interpreting the lines in a person's hand, the palmist can understand that person's potential, but can't read that person's future."

"What can you do?"

"The lines in your palm indicate your character and your destiny. At one time, palmistry was considered sorcery or witchcraft. But today, it's viewed differently. Police use a similiar science to catch criminals, don't they?"

He didn't want her to make too much sense to him, he realized. As if she didn't need a response from him, she turned away. Leisurely David regarded her legs in the tight, washed-out jeans as she strolled toward a table. A silk, bright turquoise scarf held back her hair. Coins that resembled trinkets in a pirate's loot dangled from her ears. A thick, gold chain hung into the folds of her aqua-and-pink silk T-shirt, and a bracelet that resembled a coiled snake clung to her forearm. He felt a surge of desire mixed with humor. Different best described her. So did alluring, he admitted to himself. And intriguing.

At his silence, she shot a look over her shoulder.

Dragging his eyes away from her legs, he focused on a wall chart.

"That's a diagrammatic chart of Ptolemy's geocentric astronomy," she informed him. "But you aren't interested in learning what's in your future, are you?"

"I know what's in the future."

"Do you?" She cocked a brow. "ESP?"

"Common sense. The future holds whatever I want it to hold."

"Ah."

The one sound carried both amusement and a challenge. The amusement he could slough aside. The challenge was something he'd never walk away from.

"Is that what you'll tell your brother?" she asked.

David whipped around. "My brother?"

"Matt is coming home for a visit, isn't he?"

She'd heard gossip, David assured himself. How else would she know? "Yes."

"And you're worried about him?"

"It shows?"

She merely smiled.

"During a phone call several weeks ago, he hinted that he might not go back to college in the fall. He wants to spread his wings."

"He's young."

"Twenty."

"That's young, David."

"He's acting irresponsibly."

If he was annoyed with her, he kept the emotion firmly restrained, she noted. "Why do you think he is?"

David toyed with an amulet hanging from a turntable display. "All he keeps saying is that he wants some adventure."

"I can understand that."

He didn't doubt that. "He needs to finish his education first. Make something of himself." He turned a medallion over between his fingers. "Is this another good luck charm?'' he asked, holding the gold beetle out to her.

"Yes." She stared at his hand. She already knew it could be gentle. Could it be demanding, too? She shifted her mind back to the moment. "Matt's the youngest, isn't he?"

David kept his eyes on the bronze of Nostradamus, a famous sixteenth-century seer. How could this woman who lived her life as if she were a butterfly, without responsibilities to anyone or anything, understand him? Understand the years that he'd been a father more than a sibling to his sister and brother? "The most difficult."

"Carolyn used to tell me that you virtually raised her and her brother."

"I was the oldest. My mother needed help." Unexpectedly she moved close and touched his arm with the familiarity of an old friend.

"David, what do you think he should want?"

"To finish school."

"And then get married? Settle down?" she questioned.

As he shrugged, his shoulder brushed hers. "That's what most people do."

Some warnings came instinctively to a woman. Jillian felt a slow one moving through her and knew that she shouldn't have asked him to come to the shop. "You're the one being unrealistic now." She stepped away from him to hang several long chains of silk threads on a counter turntable.

David had lived with his sister's moods. He felt he knew women, and he knew now that his words hadn't annoyed Jillian, hadn't made her scurry from him.

The idea that she was as attuned to an attraction as he was only complicated matters. He peered at the carved wood objects dangling from the threads. "What are those?"

"Pendulums." She'd promised herself that she wouldn't say more about his brother, but she was plagued with a trace of meddlesomeness. "You're too logical a man to believe that marriage makes a person responsible. Look at my mother. She married four times. She faced a lot of broken promises."

"Why?" he found himself asking.

"She was always drawn to the wrong kind of man."

"What kind of man?" he asked, taking a step closer.

"My mother gravitated toward staid men as if they'd supply some semblance of respectability, some predictability in her unpredictable and unusual life. Repeatedly she married that kind of man—the wrong kind for her. She never learned from past mistakes," Jillian explained. "And marriage didn't settle her down." She let out a long breath and met the dark eyes focused intensely on her. And her daughter had never learned from past mistakes, either, she mused. Why did she feel compelled to solve someone else's problems? Why couldn't she mind her own business? He was a perceptive man—too perceptive, Jillian reminded herself. If she wasn't careful, he'd see too much. "She didn't act very responsibly," she managed in a voice that sounded too soft and unfamiliar to her.

"Your mother wasn't really—"

"Normal?"

Wincing, he stopped a few feet from her. "I meant—she was different."

"Kindly said. Yes, she was different, but she wanted what any woman does. And she never found that happiness, because marriage isn't the be-all and end-all." She placed one of the pendulums on her palm and held it out to him.

"What are those used for?"

"For an ancient form of dowsing."

David pretended interest in the pendulum, but he was really studying her. She spoke lightly, but he was alert to the underlying sadness in her voice. He also sensed that she had a tarnished view about marriage. As a lawyer, he spent hours spouting arguments for clients. But he'd learned more when he'd sat back and observed. People donned masks. He wondered at the moment if she was? What would she have to hide? "Do you really believe that some people have more power than others and can see into the future?" he asked, handing the pendulum back to her.

She ran a slender hand over the glossy clear surface of a crystal ball in an almost loving gesture and avoided his question. "Do you believe a person can be bewitched?"

His lips twitched as a grin teased their corners. "No."

"In love?"

He cocked a brow. "Are you saying that they're the same thing?"

"What do you think?" she asked.

"About love?" At her nod, he grinned. "Hormones."

She couldn't hold back a laugh. "Are you always inclined toward such romantic thinking?"

He turned his back to her to peer through a glass counter at a crescent-shaped pendant. "Sometimes I fight it," he said in a deadpan voice that was meant to nudge her funny bone.

"So you're always realistic?" She caught her breath as suddenly the statue of Nostradamus floated across the room and settled on another display counter. *Dammit, Morgana.* Swearing under her breath, Jillian glanced at David, praying he hadn't noticed that the statue had moved. She barely finished the thought when he faced her.

"To a fault—" His voice broke off, his eyes shifting to the statue. Frowning, he gave his head a shake as if trying to clear a muddled thought.

Jillian rushed her words. "You were saying that you're realistic to a fault."

David dragged his eyes away from the statue. "I have a difficult time accepting what can't be explained."

She didn't want this, she insisted as she felt herself responding to his honesty, warming to him. He'd just warned her. He'd just confirmed that he was like her mother's husbands. Practical men; they'd viewed visionary ability as ridiculous. If she knew all that, why was she still drawn to him? In a defensive move, she hurried across the room to another counter.

She rushed everywhere, David mused. But her quick pace now revealed a nervousness that had nothing to do with natural energy and everything to do with sparks.

Following her, he noticed the skimpy leather straps on her feet that were a flimsy excuse for sandals. A concession to what was proper? he wondered. Did she like to go barefoot? He stared at the clear polish on her toenails. She was a contradiction. Unusual yet conservative.

Jillian scooped up tarot cards and shuffled them. She needed to read them later. She needed some confirmation that she was overreacting whenever he was near.

"Do you plan to read your future?"

"It's not really necessary. They'll probably tell me to watch out for lawyers."

"Is that so?"

She responded with a laugh.

He listened to the soft, smooth, sensuous sound and felt a jolt course through him that was unsettling. Because he'd schooled himself to maintain control over everything, especially his emotions, he blamed the reaction on mixed signals. One moment he felt a warmth and comfortableness with her that represented friendship. The next moment she seemed guarded and strained as if they were strangers. David turned to study another chart. One kiss might make the difference. The unknown was always intriguing, he reminded himself.

He continued to stare at the chart. "That's known as Mansions of the Moon," Jillian offered. "It shows the zodiac," she said before turning her back to him.

While she rearranged books on a shelf, David stared at her slender back, at the strands of glistening red hair. One thought filled his mind. He wanted her. The quickness of desire made no sense to him. Had years of penned-in emotions crept to the surface? Or was curiosity leading him? He tried to concentrate on something, anything but her, and stepped closer to the chart to decipher it. On a nearby shelf were bottles of colored water. David glanced at one filled with a clear blue liquid.

"It's a love potion."

He turned slowly. Her back was still to him. How the hell had she done that? She'd snuck a look, he decided. She'd had to. But as she faced him, he was caught up in confusion. In the blue eyes meeting his, he saw vulnerability. Fear. Uncertainty. Though he prided himself on being intelligent and quick on his feet, she was baffling him. "A love potion?"

Her heart thundered as if it might burst through her chest. She hadn't meant to reveal anything. She was usually so cautious. But maybe this was for the best. He'd think her weird. Wasn't that always her shield to keep men at bay? "Nothing you'd be interested in," she said in a forced, teasing tone.

David continued to stare at the bottles with their colored liquid, but he never lost sight of her. She was a strange combination. Mystical sorceress? Or shrewd businesswoman? "Do you think you should play with fate by selling these?"

"They're harmless."

David looked up. "So you don't believe in any of this?"

Her chin raised a notch. "If I didn't, I wouldn't sell them."

She gave him the aloof, annoyed look of a regal princess. David stifled a grin. "Then how can they be harmless? What if you slipped some of the love potion in Clarence Bessinger's morning tea and the first person he delivered mail to that day was Agnes?''

At his tease, tension eased from her. "A calamity would occur," Jillian returned with a laugh.

"What if we both put a drop or two in our coffee, what would happen?"

"I wouldn't open that one," she warned as he tried to open the bottle.

"Will I fall in love with your cat?"

"Macavity?"

At the sound of his name, the black cat's tail twitched.

So she had named the cat after the clever one in a T.S. Eliot poem. Who was she? he wondered not for the first time. "Unusual name."

"Did you know that Eliot was fascinated by the tarot symbols?" She brushed a strand of hair away from her cheek. "The 'wicked pack of cards' in *The Waste Land* refers to the tarot cards."

David looked up from his struggle with the cork on the bottle.

Noting his white-knuckled grip on the cork, she cautioned, "David—don't. That potion has a terrible—"

As the cork popped, he reared back with a grimace. "Jeez."

"Smell," she finished, stifling a smile.

"What is this made with? Wet shoes left in a gym locker?"

Amused as much at his need for an explanation as at his humor, she gave in to the smile. "What's your sign, David?"

He squinted at her as if she'd asked him some unfathomable question about the universe. "I have no idea."

"What's your birthdate?"

"December 28."

"A Capricorn."

His lips curved in a slow, crooked smile. "Is that good or bad?"

"Good for a lawyer. I thought that you might be."

He shot a look at the horoscope chart on the wall near him. "What did you say yours was?"

"Aquarius."

With a step forward, he peered at the chart. "According to this you're idealistic and brainy. Is that true?"

"The sign of a nonconformist. A lover of freedom," she answered. "So do you like the shop even though it's odd to you?"

He swept a look around it. "It's one of a kind. Any ghosts?"

"Maybe."

He narrowed one eye at her.

"Something of everyone who's ever lived here remains."

"Such as?"

"Such as Grandpa Mulvane's hazel twig, Grandma's tea-leaf cup, Mama's crystal ball, Aunt Morgana's runes."

"Runes?"

"Letter symbols of an ancient alphabet. After a heartbreaking love affair, Aunt Morgana went to Sweden for several months. When she returned, she became known for 'casting the runes' to predict the future."

She raked a hand through tousled strands in a tell-tale, nervous manner that belied her carefree manner David noted. "Does predicting the future help avoid problems?" he asked.

"Sometimes."

"But not the problem Riley caused?"

Her brows drew together. "Agnes is upset with me these days." She sighed heavily. "And she's enticed some friends to help. A friend of hers is my neighbor, Lillian Hilden. She filed a complaint about my running a business out of my home."

"Is that why Riley was here?"

"Yes. With Lillian and his cousin Agnes nagging him, I'm not surprised he rushed over to tell me."

"Tell you what?"

"That another complaint had been filed by Lillian. And well, you must have heard about—"

"Others," he finished for her.

"Yes, I'm sure you have." Absently she toyed with the charm bracelet on her arm. "At the town council meetings?"

"Yes."

She sighed. "I'm being politely asked to find a new shop. I hate to do that. The house is perfect."

He smiled at her words. Her perfect house was a brooding monstrosity with a sinister ambience.

"But," she added with a shrug, "to keep peace, I'll have to look for a building. That won't be easy. But I'd settle for anything, even an abandoned shack. Property has gotten really expensive in Lakeside."

As he worked his way back to her, she felt uneasy. Frightened? she mused. Of him or herself? Both, she realized. The attraction had never vanished. "Summertime is madness here now, isn't it?" she rambled, not wanting the silence to lengthen. "People are always flocking here with their motor boats."

"So where are you going to look for a building? Near the craft shops?"

As he stood beside her, she inwardly tensed. "Too commercial. But I'm optimistic by nature. It's a trait of my sign."

She had to be, David thought. In one day, her brother had been arrested and she'd been informed that she needed a new location for a successful business. He hoped that she maintained that bright, sunny attitude tomorrow. "About everything?" he asked, never recalling any woman raising his curiosity so much. Was it because she was different? Because she emanated such vibrance and enthusiasm? Because she enticed while challenging everything he'd ever believed in?

While she nervously straightened several bottles on a glass counter, temptation led him. In a slow stroke, he ran a fingertip across her throat to her pulse. It hammered wildly.

Jillian stood still, but her heart raced. Hadn't she always worried that she would become interested in someone who would never accept her as she was? Her mother had never met a man who'd felt comfortable with her eccentricity. She wouldn't let it get out of hand, she promised herself. She'd protect herself. "On some days, it's possible that a person's higher consciousness and the energies of their upper spheres aren't unified." Instead of looking baffled or wary by her deliberate prattle, he offered a smile that Jillian could only interpret as amused.

His eyes captured hers. "What happens when everything is unified?"

"Anything is possible," she said softly.

"Like what? Is that when a person gets a new job? Or an attraction begins?"

"It's possible that you might become attracted to..." Her voice trailed off as he toyed with a strand of hair near her ear. She'd known a man's casual, and his intimate, touch before. So why was the caress of this man's hand making her nerves jump? "But you're a reasonable man, aren't you?"

The fiery strands fell around his fingers like a seductive web. Soft, scented, the strands lured him to bury his face in them. "What are you?"

She tried to think of all the reasons why she should push away from him. Instead, she found herself leaning closer. He had the ability to cast a spell of his own. An intoxicating one. "I believe in following intuition."

"And do you always follow it?"

Her sigh slipped out as his lips teased her earlobe. Pleasurable shivers shot down her spine. She loved the unexpected, the unpredictable, but he was the last person she'd have pegged as susceptible to whims. She said the obvious. "David, I don't know what this is all about but—" She paused to draw a breath. "You're the kind of man who has his future all mapped out. Isn't there some chosen woman?"

"At the moment?" he murmured, fanning her ear again with his warm breath. "Yes." He tightened his arm on her back and turned her toward him. "You."

The eyes staring at her were serious. Clinging to a sanity that she felt was perilously close to slipping away, Jillian pulled back.

He caught her arm, halting her before she could take a step away. "What will happen if I buy one of these?" he asked with a glance at the love potion bottles.

Her heart pounding, Jillian looked back at him. "Nothing catastrophic," she answered, determined to rely on wits and keep the moment light.

He studied her for a moment. She stood still as if frozen to the spot. Filtered light from the beveled-glass window shadowed a lacy design over the pale skin of her neck. She looked delicate. Angelic or other-worldly? he mused. "What? Love at first sight?"

She raised her eyes to his. "Perhaps."

"A kiss?" he said so softly that her knees weakened at the sound.

"It depends."

"On what?"

"On how receptive we are to the spell."

His mouth hovered close to hers. "Are you?"

She tried not to let her body soften against his, but when he pressed his lips to the corner of hers, she felt herself melting. "The potion might overwhelm," she managed.

"But I don't believe in fortune-telling."

"Then taking the potion would be crazy." She realized that she was trying to reason with him. When had the turnabout happened? When had she become the practical one? she wondered but was suddenly aware that the hand she'd placed on his chest to push him away was sliding upward toward his shoulder. When had her resistance dissolved? Beneath her palm, she felt the quickened beat of his heart. "And you don't believe in mind reading, either, David—"

Lightly his mouth roamed across her cheek and then back to her mouth. "Lips. I read lips," he said softly. As her mouth relaxed beneath his, he caressed the side of her face. He wanted to linger and savor the velvety soft texture, but he felt caught up in something unreal. Maybe he'd resisted her softness before this moment knowing that one kiss could be addictive. He knew he should pull back. But the thought was fleeting. He tugged her closer and tangled his fingers in her hair. She was different from others. Her kiss made him instantly think of heat. When he slipped his tongue into her mouth, she welcomed the invasion. She was fire. She was a sorceress who weaved a spell, he reflected, aware that her taste wouldn't be easy to forget. But that wasn't because of some mystical hocus-pocus. What he was feeling had nothing to do with supernatural magic. For too long, he'd wondered about this woman. As her mouth teased and played with his, her scent aroused desire, her hands gentle and exploring on his back enticed him. She was a sweet witch who could weaken him with a mere kiss.

Jillian had no idea if she was tempting fate. She only knew that the mouth on hers was warm and sweet. And more persuasive than she'd ever imagined. For so many years, she'd wondered about his kiss. She'd thought it would make her heart race. She'd expected it to make her legs feel numb. Then she'd told herself that one kiss wouldn't do any of that. She'd grown up. She'd been kissed by other men. None of them had ever stirred even a minor explosion within her. Even Jason, the one love in her life, whose mind she'd fallen in love with, had stirred only a flicker of warmth. So why was David's kiss rocking her as if she stood on ground that swayed with some unexplainable force? As if he felt the same sensation, he tightened his hold on her.

Patiently his lips teased and nibbled hers. She breathed in the sharp, spicy scent of his after-shave. She strained against him. He murmured something unintelligible. She didn't care what he'd said. An urgency, a desperation for more was beginning to build within her.

Fighting herself Jillian wavered between deepening the kiss or tearing her mouth from his before all thoughts fled. But he made her want, she realized. He made her want something that she'd given little thought to in a long time. Only with Jason had she considered more than a cursory relationship. Other men had offered no complexity, no mystery. She'd been bored. Here was a man who would challenge, who would make life interesting. Here was a man who stirred desire with a kiss. Here was a man who was definitely wrong for her, she remembered, forcing herself to take a step back.

"I really didn't expect that to happen," he said softly. He reached out and caressed her cheek. "Maybe it should have years ago."

She watched the door close behind him. Tingle. She was tingling all over. A silly but unmistakable reaction for a woman close to thirty. The accelerated beat of her heart sent her flying toward the tarot cards. She'd concentrate on them. They'd tell her that those moments were quick, enjoyable ones to delight in for an instant. They would assure her. They would remind her that he was too conservative for her. He was too earthbound. Her mother had married four men similar to him and had lost. Jillian knew that she needed a man who looked toward the stars. David stared at the ground, always making sure his feet were firmly planted. They were from two different worlds.

Jillian sighed with annoyance, aware that none of her reasoning had helped. With one kiss, David had shaken her world.

She looked up to see the bronze statue floating back to its original position. Jillian muttered an oath. She didn't need a meddling, do-gooder ghost interfering. She had enough problems.

Chapter Four

She wouldn't make too much of that kiss, Jillian promised herself the following morning. As she approached the courthouse, she saw David standing outside and vowed again to keep their relationship casual. They'd discuss Andy, but she wouldn't allow a repeat of what happened yesterday afternoon. Winded, she stopped beside him on the steps. "Am I late?"

David glanced at his watch. "Five minutes to go. Did you come on your bike?" he asked, slipping a palm beneath her elbow.

"It's being repaired. I ran a block to get here on time." She slipped her arm free of his warm grasp. "I stopped at a real-estate office this morning."

"Any luck?"

"Not yet. The most difficult part of my day was setting the Closed sign in the window and knowing it was there forever. I felt as if a piece of my life had just slipped away. But I'll find something else. Carol, the real-estate agent, doesn't think we'll have a problem. So?" She looked up at him. "What should I do today?"

"Just sit in court and smile encouragingly at Andy. I have some good news. I checked with the telephone company. According to them, the phone number that Siverson gave Andy is for the Pizza Palace in Farleyville."

"That's only twenty miles away."

He merely nodded.

"In our county?"

Again, he nodded.

"Did you know that I love pizza?" She grinned. "I might just try the Pizza Palace's specialty."

"Somehow I knew you'd say that."

"Reading minds now, counselor?"

His fingertip outlined her lips lightly. "It's my second choice."

Excitement skittered through her. It annoyed her. "David, don't—"

"Don't what?"

She ignored his rarely seen boyish grin. "You know," she added as she started climbing the steps.

"Jumpy, Jillian?"

She slanted a look at him. "You seem to be."

David stifled a laugh.

"You should have had ginger tea this morning," she suggested.

"Why?"

"Because ginger is good for you. It relaxes and settles nervous stomachs."

At the sound of car tires on the courthouse parking lot behind them, David looked back. "I don't have one."

Jillian noted his frown at Agnes's car. "Yours is tense."

"No, it isn't," he countered.

"Of course it is," Jillian went on. "You're a lawyer. All high achievers have tense stomachs."

"I'm perfectly relaxed."

"Then why are you gritting your teeth?"

He sighed heavily. "You're making me do that."

"How could I do that?"

"Never mind," he said.

"You have to relax, or it will weaken your confidence," she went on. "But I can tell you what to do to remedy that."

"Please don't."

"It's quite simple. And no one will know."

He placed a hand on the doorknob but stopped. She stood very straight beside him, confident looking. He wanted to scoff at her silly superstitions, take a stand that he didn't believe any of them. Instead, staring at her mouth, he could only think about the sweetness of her taste. And he ached with an impulsiveness foreign to him to grab her by the shoulders, yank her close, kiss her again, and say to hell with what people thought. "I'm going to hate myself for asking this. But what will no one know?"

"That you're building confidence from within."

He nearly grinned. "I'll bite. Tell me how."

"Are you wearing anything red?"

He didn't need time to consider the question. "No."

"There you are. You need to wear red. Red is a confidence builder."

"I've never worn red in court."

"You should. It would help you be even more successful." She shoved her purse at him. "Here, hold this?"

"Hold—" David glanced around as he dangled the oversize canvas handbag with its embroidered zodiac signs. "I guarantee that carrying your purse into court isn't going to boost my confidence," he said on a laugh as he accepted the moment as an amusing one.

Her head bent, she fiddled with the knot of her sash. He was a good sport, she realized. She found that thought as disturbing as every other one she'd had about him. She didn't want him to be too charming. As she looked up from untying the knot, she met his eyes. They were the softest brown eyes she'd ever seen. They gentled a face that bore a hard, no-nonsense look most of the time. "Here." She whipped off the sash, offered it to him, and beamed.

David stared down at the silk scarf in his hand. "You don't expect me to wear this?"

"Oh, no."

He breathed with relief.

"Just ball it up and stick it in your briefcase or a pocket. Whenever you feel your confidence waning, touch it. The courage of the color red will send a signal through your hand and up to your brain and—well—voilà! You'll feel confident."

What he felt was warm, he mused. Her fragrance clung to the fabric. He resisted the temptation to bring the scarf to his nose and deeply inhale a scent that made him think of her. "Red is a good color, huh?"

She smiled. "According to color coordinators. But sometimes, red, like in the clouds of a crystal ball, means trouble or danger." A satisfied look settled on her face as he shoved the scarf in his pocket. "Now we can be confident that—"

Before she could finish, he flung open the door and urged her into the courthouse. "Do me a favor and have confidence in Andy's lawyer, not a red scarf. Okay?"

Too much about him made her want to relax, be herself. But she knew better. People expected her to make crackpot comments, and she'd used that image to her advantage most of her life. Now more than ever, she needed the protectiveness of eccentricity that no practical person would accept, especially someone like David. "I do have confidence in you. But I knew before I came that everything would be fine today." She led the way toward the courtroom. "I bowed nine times toward the moon last night."

David grabbed her arm, stopping her. "You did what?"

"I shook silver coins in my pocket."

"No, you said something about the moon."

"I did that, too. For good luck." Suddenly she frowned.

What now? he wondered and resisted glancing around to see if a black cat was behind him. "What's wrong? Did my luck vanish?"

"No." Jillian struggled to stifle a grin. He looked so serious, so confused. "A confident image can only stretch so far, David. To be on the safe side, you might want to give my purse back to me.''

"I told you everything would be all right.'' Jillian beamed as they stepped outside nearly an hour later and waited on the steps for Andy.

Not for the first time, he noticed green specks in her blue eyes. They made him think of the ocean shimmering beneath sunlight.

"What do we do now?''

"*I'll* do some checking. We need to find some other automotive parts dealer who did business with Siverson.''

"So we go to other towns?''

"I go.''

"I go, too,'' she insisted. "I need to be involved in this. He's my brother, David. I can't sit back and do nothing. Could you?''

She'd zeroed in on his weakness. He'd have done anything to protect and to help his brother or sister. Still, he narrowed his eyes at her, hoping to dissuade her. He could accomplish more alone.

"Is that the look that you used to give your brother and sister?''

"It doesn't work, huh?''

"No. I'm helping,'' she said firmly.

David acknowledged that he'd met his match in obstinacy. "Then I won't bother arguing.''

"Good,'' she responded, looking up as Andy came out of the doors.

Grinning, he hurried to them. He drew a deep breath. "You don't know how great it feels to smell fresh air. I didn't think that they'd keep bail that low.''

Jillian linked an arm with his. "We have a good lawyer." She flashed a smile at David then turned back to Andy. "You won't go through that again, Andy. I promise. David and I are going to find Siver—"

Jillian's words broke off as she saw Agnes standing at the top of the steps like a reigning monarch. Her dark auburn hair with a touch of gray at one temple was sleekly wound into a chignon. Disdainfully her blue eyes flicked over Jillian before zeroing in on David. Beside her, like a maid in waiting, Lillian Hilden copied her friend's pose and lifted her chin in a snubbing fashion. She was a small and frail gray-haired woman. Nervously she ran a smoothing hand over the sleeve of her blue polyester dress.

"David, I'd like to talk to you. *Alone*," Agnes insisted.

Jillian heard his whispered curse.

"Why don't you two go to the car." He handed his car keys to her. "I'll join you in a minute as soon as I'm done talking to—"

"Dragon lady," Jillian whispered. "Come on, Andy. Let me tell you what happened yesterday."

"Was it good?" he asked, turning with her to descend the stairs.

"Let's say today has got to be better," she answered lightly.

His day wasn't going to be, David thought as he faced Agnes and her friend.

"I received the letter from your office two days ago concerning the matter of Jillian's house. Why didn't you call?" Agnes demanded.

"Your request required an official, legal response."

Her frosty eyes never strayed from his. "My request requires action. I provide you with a sizable retainer, David. I expect preferential treatment."

"Are you really getting involved with *them*?" Lillian interjected.

David stifled the rude response riding his tongue. "Agnes, before I left on vacation, I checked on land deeds as you requested."

"So your letter stated."

"You can't get the Raven Lane house. It legally belongs to Jillian."

"That house once belonged to the Simpsons." Her smooth voice thinned with annoyance. "I want it back."

"That whole block of houses on Raven Lane once belonged to your husband's family. It doesn't now. Jillian Mulvane has the deed to that property. You own all the rest, except for Mrs. Hilden's home," he said with a glance at Lillian. "Why would you want the Mulvane house?"

"I want it," Agnes cut in.

David grabbed a peppermint from his pants pocket. He needed something to sweeten the moment.

"Make her an offer," Agnes commanded.

"On the house?"

"Yes, on the house. I told you. It belonged to the Simpsons. It will again," she said firmly before whipping around and storming away.

"She wants it," David muttered around the piece of candy in his mouth.

Jillian guessed David had met the siege without being harmed. But as he walked toward the car, she noted the tenseness in his face. "How is Agnes?" she asked when he'd settled behind the steering wheel.

David shoved the key into the ignition. "She was breathing fire."

For a second, Jillian considered his mood. Guessing that he'd rather forget than discuss his encounter with Agnes, she leaned toward the dashboard. She decided to try to lift his spirits. "Look at that cloud," she urged, pointing up at the sky.

David draped his arms over the steering wheel. "Which one?"

"The little wispy-looking one," she said. "It looks like a butterfly."

"A moth."

She frowned. "A butterfly." Like a child, she continued to stare upward, smiling.

How long had it been since he'd taken the time to guess the shape of a cloud? he reflected. Not since he was ten.

She settled back on the seat. "Andy is picking up a tent. I have a booth at the festival tomorrow."

"I'm glad Andy isn't here."

"Is there another problem?"

"For me there is."

She inclined her head. "What is it?"

"I talked to the sheriff. He reminded me that if Siverson had sold stolen parts to other dealers, someone would have reported him."

"Why would they? Maybe they're selling the parts, and like Andy, they don't know that they're stolen."

"The sheriff had Riley call several of them. No one has heard of Siverson. Are you sure that Andy isn't lying to you about Siverson?"

She gave him a look that might make a weaker man shudder.

He laughed. "Are you hexing me?"

"Don't you dare say it," she said softly, appealingly. "Andy is telling the truth. And he needs all the support he can get. Now I have to go to the town square and set up my booth. Then I have to pick up my bike, and—"

David held up a halting hand. "Name one place, and I'll drive you there."

She wanted to say no. But she recalled his sister, Carolyn's complaints years ago. "No one changes his mind when he's set on doing something." There were many ways to discourage a male, Jillian mused. For both their sakes, she had to. She saw in him too many qualities that she'd sworn to avoid in any man. The big problem was that in him the qualities seemed to enhance an attraction. "Okay," she answered, "but are you going around the town square from the west?"

David sent her a quizzical look. "I planned to."

"Well, make sure you approach the fountain from east to west on the south side." She noted puzzlement in his eyes. "It's bad luck to go the other way," she said simply. At the quick narrowing of his eyes, she guessed that he was reaching his limit of patient understanding about her ridiculous superstitions. She hoped so. Though Andy needed him in his life, she didn't. She'd gone out of her way to spout off wacky superstitions all morning.

"Repeat that," he requested.

Her brows pinched with a frown. "Repeat it?"

"Yeah." He saw confusion sweep across her face. It served her right, he decided. He'd spent enough time yesterday with her to know that her superstitious nature, though fascinating, was also a phony act. At the moment, he was puzzled by it. "Repeat the directions," he said again. "So I do it right."

Jillian had put off several other men with the same act. They'd run as if they'd seen an assembly of ghouls. She concentrated, not on Andy or the vanishing Siverson. Andy would be all right. He was innocent. Siverson would be caught. He was guilty. She believed in justice. But David wouldn't be quite so easy to handle.

Peppermint-striped tents lined the length of the town square. A banner announcing the Founder's Day Festival was stretched from one towering oak to another. On the other side of the gazebo, workers carted metal bars and plastic seats toward the midway.

Jillian looked away from the Ferris wheel. She'd loved riding it as a kid. Spotting a gray-haired man standing behind a skirted table, she waved. "What are your prizes this year, Luke?" she yelled.

"Pandas." His eyes twinkled. "But you might as well take one now." He winked at David. "She should have been drafted by the Dodgers," he said, offering her several baseballs.

Jillian shot an impish smile at David. "Are you still good at this?"

He eyed the pyramid of plastic milk bottles. "Want to wager?"

Saucily she led the way to the table. "What's the bet?"

"Lunch."

Jillian slanted a look at him. "I'm not sure this is fair."

He grinned. "Why not?"

"Why not?" she mimicked. "You know why not. I didn't play third base for the Lakeside Bulldogs."

David laughed, his gaze following the gentle sway of her skirt. She was feminine. Eccentric. A woman who'd constantly offer surprises.

"You didn't play in college, did you?"

Pacing himself for her stride, he walked beside her. "How do you know that I didn't?"

"Carolyn."

"Ah, Carolyn again."

Jillian stared at the bottles. "She was a chatter-box."

He smiled. Few people knew that except her family. Leaning a hip against the table, he watched Jillian aim at the milk bottles. The look of concentration on her face was as intense as a youngster who'd come upon his first anthill. "Are you going to throw or stare at the bottles all day?"

She narrowed her eyes at him. "Are you trying to distract me?"

"How long does it take to warm up?"

She bounced one ball in her palm. "I have a feeling that you're not a gracious loser," she jibed and tossed the ball. The bottles toppled. "She sent me a photo of Sam and Amy."

Beginner's luck, David mused. "Cute kids."

"You aren't prejudiced, are you?" she teased while the old man set up the bottles again.

David noted that a smile lingered on her lips despite the intensity in her expression as she prepared to throw again. "No, I'm only their uncle," he answered, frowning at the bottles strewn on the ground for a second time.

"Carolyn said that Sam wants to be just like you."

"Correction. Johnny Bencho and me."

"You're responsible for that."

He sent her a questioning look.

"You sent him the baseball mitt, didn't you?"

A warm pleasure moved through him that she'd cared enough about Carolyn to keep in such close touch with her. "Amy gets one next year," he said on a laugh.

She tossed the third ball and then grinned as the bottles scattered.

"That was amazingly lucky."

"Skill," she countered.

"One panda for the lady," Luke announced, offering the stuffed animal to her.

Jillian shook her head. "Give it to a little one, Luke." She turned to David. "Your turn."

He slapped a bill on the table. "I'll pass. Here's a donation." Slipping a hand around her arm, he urged her toward the row of tents. "Which one is yours?"

Jillian pointed. "That one."

"I'll be back in a few minutes."

Jillian sent him a puzzled look.

He leaned forward and kissed the tip of her nose. "I owe you lunch. I lost."

His hand glided down her arm. A shock wave skimmed her flesh. Watching him stroll away from the tent, she reminded herself that years ago she'd allowed her guard to drop. She'd left herself open and vulnerable to hurt. Jason had taught her a lesson that she couldn't afford to forget.

Alone in the tent, she dug into the task at hand. She believed in doing jobs quickly, even housecleaning, to finish before drudgery set in.

She unpacked the one crate that she'd asked Andy to pick up for her. The warmth of a noonday sun beat down on the top of the canvas tent. Beads of perspiration dotted her upper lip. With a soft groan, she pushed two tables together for displaying items from her store. For the palm reading, she needed only a card table and two chairs. Lugging the folding chairs to the table, she felt David's presence even before he spoke.

"Here we are."

The strong scent of onions accompanied him. "What did you get?" she asked, eyeing the box in his arms.

"A gourmet meal."

Siding up close to him, she watched him unpack plastic stemware from the carton that he'd set on the table. She arched a brow when he fanned a tablecloth across the folding table. "I see that this is an elegant affair."

"And disposable."

"You turn a woman's head."

When she sighed for effect, he looked up with a grin. "And now for lunch."

A giggle tickled the back of her throat as she stared at the table again. "I really am impressed."

"You impress easily."

"You bought my favorite."

"Somehow, I guessed you were a sucker for the all-American hot dog."

"If it's junk food, I love it..." Her words trailed off as he handed her one long-stemmed yellow rose. Her pulse wasn't racing, she told herself. But she avoided looking at the rose. Roses meant romance. "Why—" She paused and pointed at the flower.

"A yellow one suits you."

"David, you—"

"You don't like roses?"

"I love them," she admitted.

"Any superstitions about them?" he teased while doling out packets of catsup and mustard.

"Dozens," she answered, unable to resist inhaling the flower's fragrance.

He raised his head and stared expectantly at her.

"I can't remember any of them." With his grin, she acknowledged how dangerous he really was to her heart. She thought he was a predictable man, and he kept surprising her with the unexpected.

"Who taught you all those superstitions?"

"My grandmother. She believed in many of them. And they played havoc with her life. She was weighed down with worry, always fearful. Nurturing such idiosyncrasies motivated her toward unacceptable behavior. People laughed at her because she made a fool of herself."

Despite her critical words, he heard affection in her voice.

"But she was a wonderful old woman."

David held a chair for her. "It's not easy growing up in a town where people don't think highly about your relatives, is it?"

"I didn't care."

David frowned. "How could you not?" He damned himself immediately. He'd allowed old memories to sneak through. But they were hard memories to forget. Shame and humiliation had followed after his father had left.

"Too many people in my family were unusual. I had to learn to accept what they were. People talked about them all, especially my mother. She was famous around town for speaking to dead people."

David poured a soda into her glass. "Her séances gave people food for thought."

"People laughed at her," Jillian corrected him while she squirted a line of mustard down the bun. "I can't blame them. She always talked about being a transmigrating soul, about her spirit seeking universal oneness."

"If she wasn't successful then—"

"She held séances for close friends. She knew their secrets. She helped them."

Skepticism rushed forward. David bit into a hot dog to keep himself from saying more than he wanted.

"Lucy Wilmette was mourning for her husband for over a year. After my mother held a séance and Ted Wilmette talked through Mama, assuring Lucy that he was happy and at peace, she went on with her life. Two years later, she remarried."

"She probably would have without the séance."

"Perhaps," Jillian said. "But I saw the difference in Lucy. I knew what Mama was doing. She wasn't a charlatan. She was a loving woman, who gave too much of herself to other people, including her husbands. She'd start out so happy with them, but they wanted her to change. She tried and grew unhappy until she was alone again, until she was able to live her life her way.''

''She did hold the 'most married award' in Lakeside.''

''All because she'd looked for orange blossoms and happily ever after. And all she ever got were broken promises. She thought love solved all of her problems. Instead it created a set of new ones for her. She always thought that she'd chosen wisely. She wanted a man who was stable and responsible and practical. But she couldn't be happy with one. For a while she was, but he'd expect things that she couldn't deliver, and she'd begin to feel suffocated.''

David finished chewing. ''She wanted freedom?''

''Not really. Not in the sense you mean. She needed someone who understood her. But she always chose a man who lacked imagination, who thought she was silly and her daughter was harebrained because she stared at constellations instead of studying her algebra.''

David looked up. ''Her husbands must have known that she was different. After all, she had that shop.''

''They should have,'' she agreed.

''But they didn't?''

''None of the men ever understood her. And, either she never understood what the problem was, or for some reason, she chose not to see that she'd chosen the wrong man for her.''

''Why were they wrong?''

''She needed someone who understood that she couldn't follow the accepted path. Once the differences set in, she'd leave one man and search for the next one who might understand her. Of course, he never existed."

"How can you be sure?"

At the genuine interest in his voice, she felt a temptation to believe there was one man who might understand. Was that the fate her mother had fallen prey to? she wondered. "I can't be sure. I only know that each man must have thought that he could change her. But that was impossible."

"Why did all of you go by the name Mulvane?"

"Mama thought it would be too confusing if we all kept our father's name." She grinned, looking amused. "Could you imagine? Four children all with a different last name? So we're all Mulvanes."

"Who's Andy's father?"

"Mama's second husband. Eugene Bemeyer."

"Wasn't your mother married to some guy named Fred . . . Fred . . ."

"Tunney. Fred Tunney." She dabbed her mouth with a napkin. "He was Mama's third husband."

"I thought that he was Andy's father."

She sipped her drink. "Andy and I used to laugh that we needed a scorecard to remember who was whose child."

David measured his next words before speaking. "All of her marriages didn't end in divorce, though."

"No, not all of them."

"She might have stayed married to your father."

"Mama was only married two months to him before he died. But that marriage probably would have ended in divorce, too."

"Why do you think that?"

"Because he was even more wrong for her than the others were." She inclined her head. "You know that he went on a business trip and died in a hotel fire?"

He smiled wryly. "Jillian, we're talking about William Simpson. He was too powerful in this town not to have dozens of stories attached to his name."

His words seemed ironic to her, and she smiled.

"What's so amusing?"

"For a long time, I never knew about him. Mama believed in never looking back, so she wouldn't talk about him. But I think that he'd have been like Agnes is."

"Maybe not. If he was so stodgy, why would he have married your mother?"

She laughed suddenly, unexpectedly.

She was a woman as unpredictable as the weather, David mused. Always changing.

"According to Mama, everyone said that she'd cast a spell over him and bewitched him."

David understood. He'd begun to think the same thing about himself. "So she did talk about him?"

"Only to tell me that and his name. By the time I was old enough to ask, she was already out of love with husband number two. People talked. Because Mama was so eccentric, gossipers enjoyed the idea that she cast spells on the men. But then they were the same people who claimed that they didn't believe in such nonsense."

"What do you believe?"

"That opposites attract. Passion led my father, and she followed on a whim."

"Are you speaking out for good sense now?"

"Don't act so surprised. Sometimes it is necessary in life."

"Careful," he teased. "You'll give yourself away."

"What do you mean?"

"I might have to tell people that Jillian Mulvane isn't flighty."

She released a deep, throaty laugh but felt a nervous flutter in her stomach at his perceptiveness. "You'd be lying."

"Would I?" He shot her a mild grin. "I don't think so. You had the good sense to get Andy a lawyer."

"Being a Mulvane in this town means you need all the help you can get."

David met her eyes. Despite the seriousness of her statement, her voice was light, filled with good humor. "Agnes is your biggest foe. And that's understandable."

She wiped a napkin across her mouth. "For as long as I can remember, she's always turned her nose up at us, me in particular."

"Because of your father?"

"For a lot of reasons."

"Like what?"

"Too many to list."

He cocked a brow.

"Oh, let's see. Where shall I start? Well, to begin with, she thinks that I acted incorrigibly at my mother's funeral."

"Why?"

"Because I wasn't dressed properly. The respectful wore black and I wore a white dress, white straw hat and shell earrings."

A grin tugged at one corner of his mouth. "You had a reason, didn't you?"

She was amazed that he'd assumed she would. "They were my mother's favorites."

"That makes sense to me."

"Even if Agnes had known, my reason wouldn't have made sense to her. She doesn't like me," she said easily.

"Could be that she's worried you'll make a claim on the Simpson fortune."

Jillian giggled. "Never. She has nothing to worry about."

"You'd have a legal right. William Simpson was your father and—"

Jillian shook her head. "I have the Raven Lane house. That's enough."

"Jillian, didn't your mother ever try to get more of what belonged to her?"

"My mother never seemed to want more," she explained, sensing his lawyer's mind at work. "She could have fought for it, I suppose."

"You could," David reminded her. "You're William Simpson's legal heir."

"I think of myself as a Mulvane."

David gave her a half smile. "Just because Agnes was married to William's brother, Hugh, that doesn't—"

"David," she cut in. "I know that I have some legal rights. But I'm satisfied with what I have. I probably wouldn't even have the house if Agnes had been married to Hugh before Mama and William were married. But Mama had the house before Agnes married Hugh Simpson. When William died, all of the

Simpson wealth belonged to Hugh. I guess there was an ironclad will. So later when Hugh died, because she was his wife, Agnes got everything.''

"Your mother should have—"

Jillian shrugged. "She was already married to someone else by then."

Her shrug seemed to emphasize her mother's behavior. According to gossip, Gwen Mulvane hadn't mourned William Simpson for long.

Jillian balled the napkins and dropped them in the carton.

As she pushed herself to a stand, David shoved back his chair. Following her out of the tent, he considered her words. Though she revealed no bitterness, she must have felt something about all those men, all those fathers who'd proven less than she'd hoped for. He'd had one father that he'd lost all feeling for, and she'd had four with no better luck. He joined her at a waste receptacle. "Have you ever thought of selling the house?" Watching her lips curl up in amusement, he guessed her answer even before she replied.

"I won't sell it. Ever," she said firmly. The trash thumped as it hit the bottom of the container. "Mama loved that house. Though her marriage to William Simpson was brief, he gave her that house. For some reason, the house always was important to her. I couldn't sell." As she shook her head, sunlight played across the crown of her hair. "It's home. It's the one certainty that existed in my life."

He'd striven for certainties all his life, working hard and leaving nothing to chance or fate, not even personal relationships. He'd always determined the beginnings and endings of them. Studying her, David realized that he was losing that control. As if unable to resist, he took her hand and brought it to his lips.

Jillian caught her breath. She knew that she was her own worst enemy. Too many feelings from long ago effortlessly warmed her to him. "I'd be lying if I said that I wasn't attracted to you, David." She gave him a wry smile. "But what sense is there to this?"

"*This* meaning us?"

She nodded.

Absently he ran a thumb slowly across the top of her hand. "Why are you using common sense to firm up your argument?"

She laughed at the way he'd said it. "That's an odd question from a lawyer."

He felt a need building within him. "You're a lady of the wind, aren't you? A woman who follows the stars, who sees brightness in the future, who doesn't worry about yesterdays."

Excitement fluttered in her heart. She wanted to sound steady and in control, but her pulse mocked her as it raced at an uneven pace.

"If you are, then why question what's happening now?" As he leaned closer, the faint tang of lilacs drifted to him. "Why worry about tomorrow?"

"Because you are, David," she said, trying to ignore the quick sensation, a sweeping one that spiraled down to her toes.

"Think so?"

"I know so."

"Do you also know that I want you?" he asked softly.

She had no defense, she realized. Her voice came out a whisper. "That would be crazy. We're not right for each other. Believe me,'' she insisted, moving away from him.

"Jillian?"

She wanted to keep going, put distance between them, but she'd taken no more than six steps from him when the gray darkness descended on her. Had she not been distracted with thoughts of him, she might have battled the images. But he'd touched her hand, and she was receptive to more than the heat of his flesh. Keeping her back to him, she struggled to see nothing, but the vision flashed before her as if filmed with a high-speed camera. Headlights glared. A Jeep veered off to the left of the road. A Jeep like David's.

She shivered with a chill, though perspiration drenched her back. Desperately she wanted to walk away in silence, but in less than forty-eight hours, she'd had two visions. Were they related? Did they have to do with the man behind her? Too many questions and no answers forced her to face him again. She couldn't walk away and say nothing. "David, be careful. Be careful around your Jeep."

"What?"

She saw his bafflement. Nothing she could say would sound logical to him, so she searched for something he'd expect from her and rattled off, "Uranus, the planet of man's inventions is squared with Saturn, the planet of sorrows."

David stared after her. The lady might be cuckoo. But then maybe he was, too, he mused, staring after her. He couldn't seem to get her out of his mind.

Chapter Five

Morning sunlight peeked through the kitchen window before Jillian roused herself from the table and the teapot before her. People expected a gypsy when they entered her fortune-telling tent at the Founder's Day Festival, and she would give them one. If anything, her mother had taught her how to put on a good performance. But first she would take care of some household chores.

Her stereo on at full blast, she let the soothing tones of *Scheherazade* float through the house while she wandered from room to room with the sprinkling can. If the downstairs of her house resembled something from Merlin's castle, the rooms on the second floor that she called her own looked like a greenhouse. She had a passion for exotic plants, African violets, and cyclamens.

Plants required time and nurturing. She knew herself well enough to understand that she'd begun a love affair with them because they were something tangible that needed her.

During her youth, she'd passed too many lonely days not to need some daily task to fill the void. Oddballs weren't popular. She'd had a solitary childhood except for the companionship of her brothers. Townspeople viewed her family as too peculiar to let their children play at the Mulvane house. Then, in her teens, she'd met David's sister.

Though Carolyn Logan had come from a family that seemed as rigid in their thinking as everyone else in town, she'd displayed an accepting nature. Jillian had wondered then if, perhaps, in some sense, the Logans were kindred souls.

As Macavity curled around her leg and meowed, Jillian snapped herself from pondering about the impossible. She and David were worlds apart. They always would be.

"Breakfast time?" She bent to pick up the cat and heard a thump in the attic. Aunt Morgana was noisier and more mischievous than usual. Cradling Macavity against her shoulder, Jillian padded back toward the kitchen. The cat meowed loudly. "You're noisy today, too, aren't you? I know Aunt Morgana's not thrilled with David, but did you like him, Macavity?"

The cat's tongue lapped across her thumb in answer.

"Me, too. I like him too much." On a sigh, Jillian swung open the refrigerator door. It contained a quart of milk, one can of cat food and two containers of raspberry yogurt. "Not exactly a feast for a king," she mumbled. She stroked the top of the cat's head. "But enough to get us started on the day. You'll have to nag me more about going to the grocery store."

Macavity lifted his head to look at her.

"Yes, you. You're slipping up on your job," she said on a soft giggle. "But today, I have no time. Tomorrow," she promised after opening a can and then pouring milk into a dish.

She set the cat on the floor and hurried into the bedroom. Five minutes later, she was fully dressed and adding a charm bracelet of zodiac symbols to the two wide gold bands already coiled on her arm. With a deep throaty laugh, she stared at herself in the mirror. The gypsy lady of Lakeside stared back at her. "Madam Jilliana, let's hope you're in fine form today." Grabbing her oversize handbag, brimming with pendulums, amulets and several love potion bottles, she headed toward the door.

"Time to look into the future, Macavity," she called back to the cat. Already curled on the counter in perfect alignment with the sunlight streaming through the window, he totally ignored her. Jillian hoped that wasn't an omen of things to come. She needed to do a good business at the festival today. Money, something she considered important only to pay necessary bills, suddenly had become vital in her life. Without enough of it, she'd never find another location for her business.

David squinted against the morning sunlight and visually searched for his watch in the bedroom. Where had he set it last night? He scanned the chaos. Though organized at work, he needed a keeper at home. He squatted to see if the elusive watch was on the night-stand.

Cussing, he headed for the kitchen. Ten minutes later, with the coffee percolating, he threw a load of clothes into the washing machine and then slid into sweatpants and sweatshirt.

On the bathroom sink was the red silk scarf Jillian had handed him. Though she presented an air of un-bridled eccentricity and quirky thinking, when first impressions were set aside, she revealed a strength and determination that he admired. She only looked as fragile as a butterfly. Beneath that delicacy was a spunky lady.

David fingered the silk. As the lilac fragrance drifted upward, a knot of pleasure twisted inside him. He should give the scarf back to her. Picking it up, he knew he wouldn't. The scent on the scarf was as ad-dictive as the woman who'd worn it. David released a soft laugh at himself. When had such romantic think-ing entered his mind before? Days ago in his car when her eyes had met his, when he'd noticed the green specks in their deep blue coloring. With an amused sigh, he looked down and saw his watch. Light danced off the gold as if it were winking at him.

He set the watch next to his wallet on the dresser and headed for the basement to lift weights. Challenges came naturally to him. He viewed them as a part of life that tested man, but Jillian might be the greatest one that he would ever face. She was touching his heart, he realized, while he slid two forty-five-pound weights on each side of the bar.

In minutes, perspiration soaked his clothes. No matter how much he worked out with weights, his muscles still complained. He grunted as he pressed the bar up again.

"Who are you going through such torture for?"

David swiveled his head toward the basement doorway. His brother had grown a thick beard. Trimmed, it made him look years older than his twenty. David suddenly felt old. The baby of the family wasn't a kid anymore, not physically, anyway. But mentally he still had some irresponsible ideas.

David set down the free weights, sat up from the bench press, and then snatched a towel off the end of the rack. Burying his face in the terry cloth, he took his time, not wanting his brother's first minutes home to include a shouting match.

"Why won't you face facts?" Matt insisted, several hours later while he and David strolled along the row of concessions at the festival. "We're different."

"An obvious deduction," David quipped to himself when his brother eyed the chocolate-cheese pizza stand. "Die happy," he told him.

Matt sauntered off but paused every few minutes to talk to any female under twenty-five who looked familiar.

Settling for a cup of coffee, David stopped by the bandstand to listen to a local rock group and search the sea of faces. His eyes made contact with Agnes's. In seconds, she closed the distance between them.

"Are you making progress?"

He could soothe her or charm her. On occasion, he'd matched her intimidation. Today, though, he felt the sunshine on his skin and wanted to think only about its warmth and the way it glimmered on one woman's red hair.

"I assume you've talked to Jillian about the house."

"She's not interested in selling," he answered.

"That's absurd. She'll sell for the right price. Everyone will."

David glanced toward the tent with the zodiac symbol sign nearby. A hand in the pocket of her scarlet skirt, Jillian was leaning against a wood upright and laughing with Myra. A bright scarlet-blue-and-purple scarf was folded like a headband and tied to hang down her back. Though delicate looking, she was no pushover. She wouldn't sell to Agnes. "Why don't you talk to her?"

"I never talk to her," Agnes answered stiffly. "Never. Make another offer. Higher this time."

"She's not interested."

The woman's jaw tightened noticeably. "We'll see about that."

David stepped back to give Agnes room to pass by. Concern crept forward as he noticed that she'd stopped beside Riley.

"I see you got cornered by the prune queen," Myra quipped, suddenly at David's side.

"She's in top form."

"When isn't she? Is she thinking up some new dastardly plot?"

David gave in to amusement. "Dastardly?"

Except to make a face, she ignored his jibe. "Against Jillian or Andy?"

David followed her gaze. Andy had come to the festival with his girl. They were standing in line for an amusement ride as if he hadn't a care in the world. But David noted that Riley was nearby, watching Andy as if he was the nation's number-one criminal. "I know that Jillian hasn't heard the last from Agnes," David answered distractedly.

"Jillian is used to her."

"She shouldn't take Agnes lightly."

Myra shot him a questioning look.

"She's had too much trouble for it to be coincidental," David said.

"Sometimes you're pretty smart. Even for a lawyer."

David laughed. "You're my greatest critic."

"And praiser. But then mutual admiration is the backbone of our relationship," she added before turning away to mingle with friends.

He grinned after her and noticed a smiling, plump woman stepping out of Jillian's tent. All morning an urge to see her had nagged him.

Jillian reached back for the diet soda she'd hidden behind the crate.

"Your last customer looked pleased."

Startled at the sound of David's voice, she nearly dropped the can from her hand. Why had she thought he wouldn't come into the tent? He'd visited the Stargazer with a curiosity that amazed her. Even now she could see an inquisitiveness in his gaze as he strolled to the display table and fingered the tarot cards.

"Were you here for the parade?" he asked, not looking back at her.

She'd handle the situation. Hadn't she always in the past? Why would this time be different? She knew how to stop a man's interest in her, she knew how to protect herself. "Dutifully."

He looked back over his shoulder at her. From a cassette recorder, the strains of a violin floated a sorrowful tune through the tent. Easily he visualized her dancing to the music, her hips swaying, her feet moving in rhythm while she held her pale arms overhead and vibrated a tambourine. He could see her falling under the sensuous spell of the music, the clinging scarlet at her hips swirling to give him a tantalizing glimpse of her long, slender legs while she answered the passionate-sounding music. A warmth and excitement, a fire seemed to spread through his veins. She did this to him, he mused. She made him push aside every levelheaded thought.

"Are you interested in the cards?"

The question seemed ironic to him. *She* was all he'd been interested in for the past few days. "Curious about their meaning."

"People believe the gypsies started using tarot cards. How you spread them is important. Reversed ones are sometimes negative signs." She noted his glance at the yellow rose. She shouldn't have kept it. But it reminded her of those moments yesterday and the warmth she'd felt with his nearness, his touch.

He kept his eyes on her and idly flipped over another card. It was reversed. "Why didn't that come out faceup?"

"Laying out the cards is complicated to explain quickly." She sounded calm, but her stomach muscles tensed from the long, intense look he was offering her. Prickles of tension danced over her skin when his gaze skimmed the gentle dip of her low-cut blouse.

David wondered if beneath the blouse was a lacy wisp of cloth as fragile looking as the skin it covered.

Almost breathless, Jillian went on, "The position of each card also means something."

"Show me."

The dare in his voice was subtle, but unmistakable. Jillian crossed the floor to him and reached across the display table. "That's why the way you spread them is important." As he moved closer, her body brushed his. Heart pounding, she concentrated on the cards. She was used to being relaxed around people, moving easily, freely. But then she'd never been quite so physically aware of another person. Even Jason, who'd made her heart soar at the tender age of twenty, hadn't made her blood rush. David did both effortlessly.

As if compelled to, he trailed a fingertip down the slender curve of her neck.

A wave of emotion swept over her. "Are you paying attention?"

Laughter edged his voice. "Intensely," he murmured as the softness of her skin tempted him, and he ran his mouth along the same path.

Jillian drew back and sent him a doubting look.

"Are you good at interpretations?" he mumbled, nipping at the velvety texture of her ear lobe.

A lulling sensation as if she'd drunk too much seemed to pass over her. "No, I'm really not good at it." She nearly sighed when the moist tip of his tongue slid over the shell of her ear. "I usually know the person and want the cards to come up a certain way for them."

Without easing from her, he pointed a finger at a card on the table. "What is this?"

Her lashes fluttered. Her heart pounded. Her pulse hammered wildly. She felt weak and definitely too vulnerable, she realized. "What does the card look like?"

David refocused on the card, but his fingers continued to caress her nape. "An old man on a mountain, holding a lantern and a shining star."

"It's the Hermit." She drew a quick calming breath. "Its interpretation is that it might be a time for caution or retreat," she managed and forced herself to duck under his arm and away from him.

David grinned at her maneuver. "And this one?" He flipped over another card.

Jillian glanced at it from a distance. "The Lovers card? Its significance is directed toward love and sexual attraction. Good or bad."

"The two cards go hand in hand?"

"They could." For a moment, his eyes met hers with an unwavering stare that left her breathless. "But you aren't having a reading," she reminded him in a faltering manner. "So they mean nothing."

"Nothing?"

"Nothing," she repeated. "Unless you believe that the future can be seen."

David turned and settled back against the table to watch her while she counted several bills in a tray. Only a soft yellow glow illuminated the tent. Shadows danced on the canvas walls. He could still hear the excitement of the crowd outside, the off-key tune of the band competing with the raucous notes of a rock group, but a peaceful cocoon seemed to be surrounding him. "Have you had any luck at finding a new location for your shop?"

"Not yet. So far, what is available is either too far from town or too high in rent. But I'll find a place soon."

Such optimism, David mused. She always kept going. He liked that tenaciousness in her. He believed that people shouldn't ever give up without seeing something through. A lesson learned from his father, who'd run like a scared rabbit when trouble had begun, when life got too difficult. He wouldn't let Matt follow in his footsteps, he thought with renewed determination.

Sensitivity was a curse and a blessing. Often Jillian gauged her own mood by what she felt when talking to someone. But David was the last person she'd wanted such closeness with. Though her back was to him, she could feel his edginess. That she was becoming too sensitive to him rang out like a warning. Facing him, she knew his thoughts were on his brother. She couldn't read minds, but she'd already become attuned enough to him to feel his brooding. "You're troubled."

The unexpected remark brought a faint smile to his face. "What gave you a clue?"

Because people gave extrasensory perception little consideration, she had no trouble concealing it. She touched a fingertip to her own forehead. "A deep frown line. Are you still upset with Matt?"

"I've been keeping clear of him, so neither of us will say anything that we'll regret. He wants to take off for the River Thames and investigate the remnants of a fourteenth century retreat."

Despite his serious expression, Jillian couldn't help smiling. "He saw an Indiana Jones movie."

"All he keeps saying is that he wants some adventure."

"I can understand that."

"He needs to finish his education first."

"Some education isn't found in books."

"It won't be found while he's pretending that he's Harrison Ford, either."

"They're both handsome." She watched a deeper frown flicker across his face. The male ego always amazed her. "But then Logan men are, aren't they?"

"Are they?"

At his quick grin, she chided, "You don't need flattery."

"Everyone can use a little boost to the ego," he said, crossing over to her.

"You're a very good lawyer."

Unable to resist, he brushed a knuckle against one of the lengthy baubles dangling from her ear. "I didn't mean a professional boost."

She grabbed his hand to stop him. "You did come to have your palm read, didn't you?"

He pressed his mouth against her cheek. "What do you expect to see?"

Jillian felt his smile. "That you're single-minded."

"Determined," he said softly.

She slipped her hand free of his and worked hard not to be affected by his knowing grin, but his dark eyes dared her to deny what was beginning to seem inevitable. Passion tempted each time they were close. How had that happened in so few days? Where could it possibly lead them? She didn't want to get hurt. And she liked him too much to see him hurt, either. "Sit at the table. And Madam Jilliana will tell you all you want to know."

"Enticing."

She laughed. "It's meant to be."

Smiling, David followed her. He watched the candlelight rippling across strands of her fiery red hair, flickering over the soft planes of her face, reflecting in the sparkle of her dark eyes. She was a true enticement. She could make a man go mad with wanting.

"Your hand?" Jillian said in a questioning tone.

"What do you see?" he asked, not unaware of how smooth and small the hand was that was gently cradling his opened one.

"According to this line, you've known true contentment," she said as she stared at his palm.

"How do you know that?"

"From the lines reaching upward here." She traced a fingertip along a line on his palm. "You've obviously made one woman extremely happy at some time."

"More than one, I hope."

She grinned at his cocky response.

He wasn't a man prone to infatuation. Though he believed desire led him, he couldn't ignore softer, gentler feelings for her. Yet no amount of reasoning would push past his logic and let him accept this part of her life. She was a contradiction. He watched her steadiness, her resiliency in standing up to Agnes, her determination to make the best of everything. And then before his eyes, he saw her looking to lumps of glossy rock, and silly trinkets, and cards with peculiar drawings on them to give her answers to life's problems.

"The shape of your fingers and nails, and the position between them tell just as much as the lines do." She ran her fingertips down one side and then the other of his hand. "A square hand signifies a logical mind."

"That's not too difficult to forecast since you know me. What about yours?" He slipped his hand over hers and held it up on the table between them. "Long, slim." He stroked a fingertip along the inside edge of her little finger. "It's crooked. Is there a special meaning to that?"

Her shoulders heaved as she took a calming breath. "It's the hand of a dreamer, someone who's idealistic." She turned his palm up again and touched the fleshy pad below his little finger. "This is the Mount of Mercury. Yours is prominent."

"A good sign?"

A hint of a smile tugged at the corners of her lips. "Imperative for a lawyer. It reveals your ability to communicate with others. Your Mount of Venus is also well developed," she said, stroking the large fleshy pad at the base of his thumb. "This indicates a loving or companionable person. I see one marriage for you."

"Where do you see that?"

She ignored the amusement in his voice. She was used to it. People predictably acted amused or skeptical when she began a reading. Many changed their minds before they left. "This line that runs horizontally beneath the Mount of Mercury. That your Head Line starts near the index finger reveals you are an ambitious person who is likely to be successful."

"And this?" he asked, pointing.

She raised her eyes. "Your Heart Line."

"Tell me," he said, unable to resist reaching across the small table and touching her hair. The strands glimmered with gold. In fascination, he watched the way one red curl determinedly coiled around his finger. The attraction between them held the same kind of tightening hold on him. Each time he was with her, he felt more drawn toward her. Each time he thought that he'd be satisfied with a few minutes, he found himself wanting hours. Each time he walked away, he yearned to turn around and go back to her.

"There are key lines on the palm," she said to keep herself from making too much of the hand in her hair. "Each one is significant by its length or depth and its distance from another line. The Fate Line determines happiness and success. The Head Line indicates the person's intellectual attitude and the way that the person will react to business and personal relationships. The Heart Line is the indicator of emotion. The Life Line offers an idea of the length of life. However, crisscrossing of other lines influences it. The Sun Line provides future predictions about a person's chance for success and wealth."

His fingers closed over hers. "My Heart Line?"

"It's near the Mount of Saturn."

"Is that important?"

"Yes. It means love and sexuality go together."

He grinned. "I always thought they did."

As he leaned forward and brushed his lips across her cheek, his breath fluttered across her face like a caress. Pulling back, she narrowed her eyes and feigned a threatening look. "I can see that Madam Jilliana can help you no more."

David's grin widened at her feigned thick Romanian accent. "I have a difficult hand to read?" he teased.

"No. You kibitz too much and break my concentration."

"Does that mean I'm being dismissed?"

She looked past him. "Definitely."

David swung a look over his shoulder. Two giggly teenagers had popped their heads in the tent. "Later then, gypsy lady." He ran his fingers caressingly across the top of her hand before he pushed himself to a stand.

With a look, he made her blood warm. Why was her life suddenly so complicated? she wondered. Why did his touch cause her heart to jump? Why was he the one who made her ponder a life as normal as the next person's?

When David stepped out of the tent seconds later, he stood in indecision. Though he prodded himself to wander past the arts and crafts exhibits, his mind remained back in the gypsy tent. He saw no point in staying at the festival. Nothing else interested him.

At nine that evening, Jillian finished her last reading. She repacked the carton and then folded the small card table and folding chair that someone from the community center would pick up. As she stepped outside the tent, she stopped to slip off her sandals. Dangling them from her fingers, she inhaled deeply. The stale odors of bratwurst and pizza and beer mingled and hung in the warm air. Swinging her bag over her shoulder, she strolled toward the amusement rides and the edge of the fairgrounds.

Then she saw him.

Lounging against the ticket booth at the entrance, his face in shadows, David waited. Smiling he stepped forward and slipped the carton from her arm. "Need a ride home?"

"You're always coming to the rescue when I'm tired or in a hurry," she said, trying to brace herself for the sensations he'd repeatedly stirred within her.

"You must be sending a message," he teased.

Jillian sent him an indulgent look. "Are you claiming to be telepathic?"

"Does that involve wishful thinking?" At her grin, he touched the small of her back to urge her toward his car. "I have to stop at my place."

Jillian froze in midstep. "Not too subtle, David."

He laughed. "I haven't asked a female to see my etchings since I was nineteen."

An incredulous look settled on her face. "You didn't?"

He stifled a laugh at her expression and shrugged. "At that age, everything is worth a try. I have to stop and set out clean sheets for Matt," he explained. "He'll never find them otherwise."

She resumed walking toward his car. "I bet he will." She tipped her head back and speculated. "I bet you're a perfectionist who has a place for everything."

He just laughed in response.

He wasn't a perfectionist. Jillian stood in the hallway of his huge house and gaped. He was a clutterer. Books were stacked on the spinet and the tabletops, newspapers were strewn across the entry hall table, on

the brown tweed sofa, and tucked under a big uphol-
stered chair. Balled in ashtrays everywhere were cellophane candy wrappers. Though the house was
basically clean, he obviously didn't consider picking
up after himself a top priority of his day.

While he hurried down the hall toward the linen
closet, she scanned the paintings on the wall. One that
stretched across the wall behind the sofa was alive with
hues of blue and pink and orange. Though abstract,
the painting clearly was of the water at sunset, and it
was a tranquil scene despite the brilliance of the colors.
The same hand had done the painting of the sensuous
river that hung in his office.

"Uh, I didn't clean the kitchen," he yelled out.
"Don't go in there."

She already had.

Seconds later, he appeared at the doorway and
grinned. "Do you have an incantation for perform-
ing miracles?"

"None that clean up dishes." She leaned a shoulder against the refrigerator. "I'm surprised.
Shocked," she admitted.

"Fooled you, huh?"

She returned his grin. "Yes, you fake."

He chuckled. "When I step out of this house, I have
to be neat."

She tipped her head questioningly. "You mean at
the office?"

"Everywhere. All the time."

She considered his words. He was right. Not once
had she seen his car or his Jeep in need of a washing.
With a sweep of her hand, she asked, "Is this the real
you?"

"Don't tell."

An impish smile curled the edges of her lips as she walked with him toward the door. Jillian glanced to the side at the room off the entrance hall. "Is that your study?"

When she continued to stare into the dark room, David resigned himself to something new that he'd just learned about her. She was nosy. He reached around the door frame and flicked on the light switch for her. "Whatever you call the room with the desk."

Jillian needed little encouragement. She was curious about him. For years she'd accepted his staid image. Now she realized she'd been unfair to him. David Logan definitely wasn't one-dimensional. Though he'd decorated the house with traditional furniture, splashes of color were everywhere. Even in his den, he'd added bright-colored throw pillows and had hung bold-hued paintings. She ran an admiring hand over the surface of the rolltop desk. "An antique?"

"My mother's father's."

"It's beautiful."

"I thought you were a woman of the future?" he teased.

"I can appreciate some things from the past." On a shelf adjacent to the window were a dozen gleaming gold bells. "Who was the bell ringer?"

"My grandfather."

"Wasn't your father one, too? I remember one Christmas when I was little. He'd performed several Christmas carols on the bells during a town festival."

"Yes, Jack did it, too."

The sudden coolness in his voice warned her. Jillian strolled away from the bells. She'd needed no extra sense to know that she'd hit a raw nerve. Studying the baseball cards stacked on top of the credenza, she noted some of the cards were forty years old. "A hobby?"

"An old one. I started collecting them—" He paused. "I was six when Jack gave me a handful that he'd had as a kid."

"You don't like to talk about him, do you?"

"There's little to say. You know the story. Everyone knows about him."

Even in the shadowed light, she could see tension tightening his features. "That happened so long ago."

"Like yesterday."

She felt the dark mood slipping over him. All she could think about was touching him, helping him with a moment that he must have experienced a hundred times through the years.

"I doubt that I'll ever forget," he said softly, as if he were talking to himself.

"You were a child. Ten or eleven?"

"Twelve." He lifted one of the bells. A rich middle-C tone rang in the air.

"You must have some good memories of him?"

"I idolized him." He leaned back and settled his hips on the edge of the desk.

Eye to eye with him, she saw the control that he'd nurtured through the years, but it wasn't difficult to imagine the tears that as a boy he'd shed for a father who'd fallen off the pedestal.

"I remember days of denial. I couldn't believe that he'd done what people were saying. I saw the people who were injured. A classmate's father had been killed in the collapse of that building. Ten people injured.

Two dead. In a town this size, that kind of loss has a rippling effect. My mother suffered the most. She was suddenly an outcast in a town where she'd been born. All because her husband had been the man responsible for the collapse of that building.''

Her heart ached for him. ''David, it's so long ago. People have forgotten.''

Though his eyes met hers, they seemed unseeing. ''I haven't. I thought that he was the greatest man in the world. And I learned that he was a cheat. He was unscrupulous. He did do what they said he did. He shortcutted on the building materials. His construction company built that auditorium. It was his fault that it collapsed.''

''Do you know where he went?''

''You mean, ran?'' He released a heavy breath. ''Yeah, I learned later that he'd moved to Mexico. He wrote a letter to me after my mother died. I sent the letter back unopened. A couple of years after that I received notice from a lawyer that he'd died and there had been a will.''

She saw a man's determination in the firm set of his strong jaw, but in his eyes she noted a boy's sad vulnerability. ''Is that when you made that donation to the school?''

''He owed this town something. And with the donation, he helped his family. They deserved not to walk in shame anymore. He put his family through hell, Jillian.'' A wry, sad smile touched his lips. ''You know, for nearly a year after he left, I kept expecting him to come back. Come home to us. He just left. He ran from everything. And I always wondered how he could have told us that he loved us and then left like that. Then I realized that he'd loved no one but himself."

"David, you've made people forget."

He drew a hard breath. "I needed to do that for myself, for my mother, for everyone who had the name Logan. My brother and sister don't remember, but I was haunted by what he did. My mother and I went nowhere without being whispered about." He spoke in the strained tone of someone fighting emotion. "You don't know how many fights I got into as a kid, defending his name. Hating him for making me have to do that."

She slid her hand over his. "Then why did you?"

"Because I was his flesh, his blood." His head snapped up, and his eyes met hers again.

Jillian saw none of the usual warmth in them.

"Whatever he was, I was."

"Don't," she insisted. "That isn't true." She held his palm up. "I read your palm. I saw a good man," she assured him. As he gave her a semblance of a weak smile, she questioned, "Why did you fight for him?"

As if the truth was too painful to admit, he looked away again. "He was my father," he admitted softly.

Jillian gave him a long, searching look. She'd known him most of her life, but he'd been a stranger until this moment, she realized. During a few quiet moments, she'd learned that beneath the controlled exterior was a gentle man, a vulnerable and sensitive one. The kind of man she could fall in love with.

He hadn't meant to say so much. He'd always kept feelings about his father to himself. He'd apologized and fought for him, but he'd never allowed his own pain at that loss to be seen before. With gentle probing, she'd made him face a past that he'd vowed to forget. Yet he felt less of the old anger and bitterness suddenly.

While they drove to her house, David fought analyzing his feelings. Why he felt as he did wasn't as important as what he felt. Somehow this soft-spoken woman with her odd little quirks had opened a window for him, and he saw sunshine again.

Her house was warm and homey, the kind of place he'd have expected the town's librarian to live in, yet it was oddly decorated. An individualist, she'd chosen no theme, no continuity for her home. At the top of the second-floor stairs, he'd dodged twigs sticking out from a two-foot-high Oriental vase. On the floor beside an end table was a red, papier-mâché dragon, and on the hallway wall between the living room and the kitchen were a dozen painted masks. David stared at one with three eyes.

"My aunt—"

"The lady who tosses stones?"

"Runes," she corrected. "Aunt Morgana collected masks from primitive cultures."

David followed her into the kitchen. It was blue with statues of cats everywhere. While she poured coffee from a thermos into a cup, he settled on a straight-back chair near the trundle table and stared at the three portable television sets stacked on top of each other. All three were on and offering fuzzy reception. A laugh edged his voice. "I guess you like to watch television?"

She handed him the coffee. "So does Macavity."

"Animals can't enjoy television," he said after taking a sip of the weak-looking brew and then setting his cup on the table.

"He thinks that he can."

"Why three?" He strolled over to the televisions and began fiddling with one dial.

"It's less boring to watch them all at the same time."

"Watching three at a time has to get confusing."

"Sometimes when the cooking show—" She paused briefly as his cup floated to the sink, tilted, and the liquid was dumped. "Sometimes," she went on in a panic as his cup floated back to the table, "that happens when the cooking show, the do-it-yourself program and the green-thumb gardener show are on at the same time. One time I added dandelion seeds to the Mongolian beef."

David strolled back to the table and reached for his coffee. "If you watched only one at a time—"

As he stared into the empty cup, Jillian watched bafflement flash across his face. She rushed conversation to keep him from asking the one question that she didn't want to answer. "If I watched one at a time, I might miss something really interesting."

Still frowning, David gave her a narrowed-eyed stare. Jillian hadn't moved. At least, he hadn't seen her move. So when had she dumped his coffee? Why had she?

She watched an amused grin curl the edges of his lips. "More coffee?" she asked, giving him her most innocent look.

He responded with a shake of his head. He saw no point in pursuing the oddity of her television viewing or her little game with his coffee. More than once he'd become aware that she played a game with people. Some of her eccentricities were for show. The problem was that he couldn't tell when she was serious and when she wasn't. "Do you ever sit and listen to music?"

"Dulcimer tapes." Deciding they might be less prone to her aunt's shenanighans in another room farther away from the attic, she led the way back into the living room. Passing a stereo, Jillian flicked a switch. The mellow tones of Lionel Richie floated into the room.

David grinned, even more convinced that because people expected the odd and the unusual from her she'd nurtured the image.

Though she gestured toward the blue-and-white sofa, David circled the room. Near the sofa was a square table with inlaid tiles. On each was a zodiac symbol. A four-foot-high brass unicorn statue stood in the corner near the fireplace. A basket of knitting yarn and a partially completed afghan had been stuck in a corner. He pointed at the basket. "Do you do that?"

She lit a candle on the mantel. "I'm one of those people who can't sit still. Nervous energy, I guess."

"What else do you do to relax?"

"Search for stars, plant flowers."

He took a step closer. "That's still being busy."

"See what I mean," she said on a laugh that was stirred more by nervousness than amusement. "I'll get us something else to drink."

"I don't want anything."

She froze and slowly turned to face him.

Light from the candle danced shadows across her face. She looked ethereal. Without a word, he closed the distance between them. All day he'd been waiting for moments alone with her again. He was aching for her, he realized as he buried his hands in her thick hair, and his mouth captured hers. At the sound of her moan, the heat of an earlier fire raced through him again. Seduction wasn't new to him. But he sensed it wasn't the answer this time. Though for hours he'd thought of nothing but her and holding her like this, he felt a hesitation now, a restraint matching his hunger. As welcoming as her lips were, as soft and pliant as her firm body was against his, she wasn't ready, he realized. Her lips nipped the corner of his, and her hands skimmed over his back, but she was easing herself away from him.

He could force the moment. But he knew the fire wasn't lapping at her. The heat and the need existed, but the desperation wasn't there. David wanted it all with her.

For another moment, he savored the taste of her, encouraged by her mouth clinging to his. He heard the beating of his own heart, its rhythm steady as it pumped blood faster. Ending the moment was harder than he'd expected. When he stepped back, he ached. Her lips looked swollen from his kiss. Her eyes shuttered. He'd made his mark. But then so had she. She'd captivated him, bewitched him, he mused. She'd worked her way under his skin as no other woman ever had.

Jillian felt every uncertainty and fear that had haunted her childhood resurface. "David, you'd better leave," she said breathlessly. When he neither moved nor responded, she raised her gaze to his. His eyes were searching again as if trying to see inside her.

What barrier stood between them? he wondered. At the moment, he wasn't even sure it was one that could be crumbled. He only knew that he wanted it gone. He held her upper arms, needing even the slightest touch with her flesh. "I've talked to you. Can't you talk to me?"

"I'd like you to go."

"Why?"

The unusual roughness in his voice sent a slow-moving shiver up her spine. Old habits never died, she reflected as she sought the easiest solution to the turmoil churning within her. "We aren't on the same astral plane."

"Stop that," he said in a tone that was controlled but edged with anger.

"Stop what?"

"I'm real, dammit. Be real with me."

She nearly choked on her next words. "You don't realize what trouble you'll have if you get involved with one of those 'crazy Mulvanes.'"

He wanted to pull her close, offer comfort against the hurt that she'd buried through the years. He'd faced similar feelings of being at odds with everyone. As different as they were, they had shared a loneliness in their youth. "No, you're lovely."

"Don't," she appealed.

"And intelligent. Special." He brushed her cheek with a kiss. "Very special. Especially to me," he said against her ear.

"David, this is crazy."

"What is? Love?"

She shook her head. "Not love."

"Might be."

She pulled back. A longing intensified within her to believe in something she'd always considered impossible for her. "You'd better go."

"That's what you want?"

"I don't know what I want," she admitted on a shuddering breath.

He was torn between an angry frustration to crush her to him and a protective urge to cuddle her and offer her comfort. But he didn't know what that comfort was for. On a silent oath, he made himself back away and waited until he reached the door before he spoke again. "Jillian?"

Again a slow-moving shiver raced up her spine. She willed herself to face him.

"I know exactly what I want. You," he whispered before flinging open the door. "I want you."

Chapter Six

After David left, Jillian wanted to list the reasons why she didn't like him. But she couldn't come up with any real reasons. She liked the way he gently probed and challenged. She knew he was a skeptic, but he wasn't too narrow-minded or too serious. His laughter sprang forward quickly. And she'd felt a warmth from him that few people had ever offered her. She was beginning to enjoy his company too much, she realized. And she felt scared. Scared to believe something was possible between them.

Before she could ponder the situation any further, the telephone rang. Jarred, she answered with a distracted, "Hello."

"I miss you."

Never in her wildest imaginings had she expected that kind of greeting from David. She melted. With three words, he dissolved any resistance she'd hoped to maintain. He was everything she thought she'd never have and everything she'd always wanted. "You left five minutes ago," she said breezily, not wanting to reveal how unsettled she really was.

"I know. And I miss you," he repeated huskily.

A tremor of pleasure slithered through her. She closed her eyes and let the softness of his voice float over her. "You're insane."

"Loony?"

She suspected that he was smiling in that slow, reluctant way that she'd begun to look forward to seeing every day. "You could be considered that."

"Then we'd belong together, wouldn't we?"

"We're not loony in the same way," she attempted to say in her most serious tone but couldn't keep laughter out of her voice.

"We both like to fish."

She struggled to abate a laugh. "Yes, we do."

"And I like looking at stars. Some night when the moon is full, we'll go to the lake. We'll fish and look at stars."

Jillian laughed at his silliness. Leaning back and closing her eyes, she cradled the phone closer. "You're overworked. That's your problem."

"Ah, that's my problem."

"Yes."

"Did you ever hear of twitter pated?"

Her eyes snapped open. "What did you say?"

"Didn't you ever read *Bambi*?"

She held back the receiver and giggled. "You read *Bambi*?"

"I had a younger sister who loved bedtime stories."

He'd make a good father, she thought then frowned, wondering at having such a thought. "David, what is the matter with you tonight?"

"I told you."

"Twitter pated?"

"Uh, huh. That's what Thumper called it when Bambi fell in love."

Her heart jumped. "You're not in love."

"I'm not?"

"You couldn't be."

"Because you aren't?"

"David, you're a sensible, reasonable—"

"Sounds boring."

"Nice."

"That sounds even duller."

"I really enjoy being with you—"

"Now that's nice," he said smoothly.

Jillian frowned. "Did you trap me into that admission?"

"Not me. It takes training to trap people into confessions. Want to spend time with me tomorrow?"

"When?"

"All day." He paused and added softly, "All night."

She frowned, confused. "Have you been drinking?"

"One drink," he said in a more serious tone. "I'm going to drive around tomorrow. Want to go with me?"

"To find someone who did business with Siverson?"

"That's the idea."

"Yes."

"At nine."

"Okay." She coiled the telephone cord around a finger.

"That's a good sign."

"What is?"

"No hesitation."

"Good night," she said firmly.

"'Night, Jill."

She set the receiver back in the cradle. "You weaken me," she whispered as she headed for bed.

By ten the next morning, Jillian was getting discouraged. Visits to small automobile shops at three different towns had proved futile.

Standing beside a candy-vending machine in a square cubbyhole office adjacent to gas pumps, she yanked at several knobs while David talked to the shop owner. When she saw his approach and his thumbs-down gesture, she felt her spirits droop.

He grimaced. "No luck."

"We're batting zero." Jillian tugged on another vending-machine knob.

"Come on." He opened the door for her and slid a hand around her arm. "Let's try the next town."

Longingly she looked at the Mars Bar in the machine. "What a rip-off."

He smiled at the indignant pout on her face. "I'll buy you lunch."

"When?" she asked eagerly with a glance back.

Grinning, he urged her toward his Jeep. "In a little while."

"A little while had better be soon."

David opened the Jeep door for her but blocked her path to the seat. "Why?"

He bent his head, and his lips brushed hers. "I get nasty when I'm hungry," she murmured against his mouth.

"Fierce?"

She felt his smile and pulled her head back to look at his face. "Ferocious."

His hand skimmed her arm. "Might be interesting." Curling his fingers around her wrist, he felt her pulse hammering.

Desire merged with an emotion she'd been ignoring. She wouldn't put a name to it. But when his lips rubbed over hers, she felt a surrender taking place within her.

"Soon," he assured her softly.

A drugging, romantic mood lingered. But Jillian couldn't ignore a more basic need five minutes later. "I'm still hungry," she complained while eyeing a fast-food restaurant. "A quick meal will do." They whizzed past the restaurant.

"Let's try the next town first," he said as if she hadn't spoken.

She sighed. Her stomach was about to rumble embarrassingly.

"What made the sheriff suspicious about Andy's shop?" he asked as he drove off the main road and onto a dirt one.

Jillian twisted her head toward him. "Who knows? On Friday, Riley strolled into the shop and started nosing around. Andy said that he didn't think too much about that. Riley does occasionally enjoy the sport of harassing a Mulvane."

"Harassing?" He dug into his shirt pocket. "How?"

"Oh, nothing serious. He just wanders into my shop and strolls around, touching everything as if he expects to find a secret supply of cocaine hidden in a crystal ball, or a top-secret microchip woven into a horoscope wall hanging. He's pesty more than annoying."

David offered a butterscotch. "So he did the same thing to Andy?"

"All the time," she answered, snatching up the candy. As the Jeep tires bounced over a rut, the candy nearly flew from her fingers. Jillian held firm. "But on Friday, Riley was more determined. Andy said that he was at the shop about a half hour, left, and then came back. For three hours, he walked along shelves and checked serial numbers on parts against those on a sheet of paper."

"I wonder if he went into the stockroom in back."

Jillian shook her head while she savoringly sucked flavor into her mouth. "No," she mumbled. "No such luck. If he had, we'd have a loophole, wouldn't we?"

"Searching without a warrant. But anything on the shelves is there for the public."

For the next few moments, she viewed the passing scenery. A person could look at only so many red barns, herds of cattle and adorable sheep. Overnight, it seemed as if acres of trees had budded. Within months, the maple trees would change from green to golden yellow. She preferred the time when the leaves turned to a brilliant crimson. But as lovely as it all was, what she really wanted to see, smell and taste was a hamburger. Her stomach was hitting her backbone. "David, did you have breakfast this morning?" she asked suddenly.

"Doughnuts."

"Junk food," she murmured.

"What?"

"I had an early customer, and I didn't get a chance to eat. I'm sorry, but I can't think when I'm hungry."

"The butterscotch didn't help?"

"Hardly enough to fill a cavity."

He grinned. "One more stop."

One more stop, she mused. If he said that one more time, she'd reach closer and strangle him. No easy task, she decided as she looked first at her small hands and then at the thick column of his neck. For her, self-hypnosis was great for everything but hunger. Still, she'd give it a try. Sitting back, she closed her eyes. A plate of french fries popped into her mind. Chocolate whipped-cream pie. Cheese and crackers. Broccoli. Broccoli! She hated broccoli.

"Farleyville is five miles west. Want to go there and take a look at Siverson's Pizza Palace?"

Pizza! Jillian nodded.

David cursed softly. His arms draped over the steering wheel, he stared at the empty building with its cardboard sign—Pizza Palace. "Another dead end."

Her stomach growled in response.

"What did you say?"

If her hunger couldn't be satiated, Jillian was determined to gain something from this side trip. She gestured with her head at the dress shop next to the empty building. "I'm going in there."

"You're going to buy a—"

The car door slammed behind her.

David scowled for only a second. Why fight what he'd recognized from the beginning. She couldn't be controlled. If she chose to be outrageous or insensible, nothing would stop her. Though he offered a grin as she glanced back, he couldn't push aside troubled thoughts. What haunted her? he wondered. He'd felt the need for him in her hands, the yearning in her mouth, the desperation when her body had strained against him. But a secret made her draw back repeatedly. He'd seen vulnerability too often in her eyes to place demands on her. Patience had been learned early in life. With his sister hogging the bathroom, he'd had no other choice. Reaching under the seat for the morning newspaper, he anticipated a long wait.

As unpredictable as ever, Jillian returned to the Jeep in less than five minutes.

David noted that she hadn't made a purchase.

"The Pizza Palace never opened," she announced as she settled on the seat. "The telephone company installed the phone. But the dress-shop owner said that during a two-month period, she saw only one person go into the building."

"You went in there for information?"

She gave him an exasperated look. "Of course, why else? The woman said that a tall, thin man by the name of Earl came in once a week. She wandered over to find out when he was opening his business. He said in a week. A week passed, and she didn't see any pizza ovens delivered. She thought he acted strange. All he did was use the phone and check the answering machine."

"She never got more suspicious?"

"She minds her own p's and q's, her words not mine. She said that he never told her his last name. But he was here for a few weeks with his cardboard sign in the window. And she never even saw a pepperoni. So?" She looked at him expectantly. "Now what?"

"I find out the name of the owner of the building. He must have a lease agreement." David grinned. "You're amazing."

Though lightly said, his words made her aware of how much his opinion mattered. She leaned back and closed her eyes. How had she allowed herself to feel so much in such a short time? Or had those feelings been dormant for years? Every time she'd passed him on the street or had seen a glimpse of his smile, had she been allowing underlying feelings to strengthen?

David noticed her frown. "Do you want to eat or sleep?"

She opened an eye and then shot a look at him. "Eat. I can't concentrate if I'm hungry."

"Okay." He grinned amiably. "The next restaurant we see—"

"I saw a redbrick building that looked like a burger joint."

David switched on the ignition. "Where?"

"In the center of town." When he gave her a puzzled look, Jillian sensed the question in his mind. They hadn't driven through the center of town, so how could she know? "I've been here before," she informed him quickly and looked out the window to avoid his eyes. His stare was too intense, too questioning. When his silence continued, she glanced back at him. "It's two streets over."

He gave her a long, steady look but said nothing.

Uneasy, she forced conversation as they strolled toward the restaurant. "They have great hamburgers here."

David slipped an arm around her waist. "I'm a roast beef man."

"I don't know how that is," she said and prayed it was on the menu. "Guess you'll have to chance it."

Jillian took one step in and froze. On the far wall of the restaurant with its Western motif was a wagon wheel. She closed her eyes for only a second. She needed no more time than that. It was the wagon wheel that she'd seen in an earlier vision.

As the gray fog took shape before her, she steeled herself to block the vision. But an image of a child, a little blond girl, flashed forward. She was laughing. She looked happy. Jillian started to smile then stopped. Fear intruded, tensing her. She saw the wheel spinning. Over and over. She heard screams. Then she saw the little girl again. Heard her cry.

"What's wrong?" David insisted.

Through the fog, Jillian caught the sound of his voice. But she wanted to cover her ears, her eyes. She wanted to block out the images. As the pressure of his fingers on her arm drew tighter, she struggled to focus on him, but she couldn't. She stared out at the room of tables and frantically searched the sea of faces for one child's.

"Jillian?"

Her eyes stopped on a little boy. On his sister. They were both too old. Relief washed over her with the realization that the child wasn't in the restaurant.

"Hey?" David said softly.

She drew a shallow breath to battle the last wave of nausea before raising her eyes to him. She saw his concern and puzzlement and grabbed for a logical excuse. "I felt faint. I guess I'm hungrier than I thought."

"Then we'd better—" He paused as the door opened behind them. With a glance back, he gently urged her away from it.

Passing them, a woman excused herself. Her child trailed after her. A blond, blue-eyed little girl with an urchin's grin.

Jillian didn't take a moment to consider her actions. "David, there," she insisted. Not waiting for him, she hurried past the woman to grab the table by the wagon wheel.

The woman gave her a strange look. Jillian didn't care. Let the woman believe she was rude. Let David think her a world-class space cadet. If she sat at the table, the child might be safe.

Puzzled, David followed and then settled on the chair across the table from her. She looked tense as if ready to fly from the chair. He touched her hand. "You weren't kidding when you said that you get fierce, were you?" Though a token amount of humor edged his voice, he frowned because she was frowning. "Are you sure that you're okay?"

"I'm fine," she said, opening the menu.

The hamburger she ordered lumped in her throat. Through the meal, Jillian kept an eye on the wheel, expecting it to fly from the wall at any moment.

"Bad hamburger?" David asked while pushing his plate away.

Jillian looked up.

Though her eyes met his, they seemed unseeing. When she didn't respond, he looked for any conversation to fill the strange silence that had stretched through the meal. "The roast beef was passable."

Jillian gave herself a mental shake and managed a weak smile.

"Do you feel better?"

"Much," she assured him. She noted his glance at her half-finished plate and then eyed an ice-cream soda at the next table. "I should have ordered that instead."

"Want it?"

"No," she answered quickly.

Concern for her gnawed at him. Even when she wasn't smiling, she was usually animated. Ever since they'd entered the restaurant she'd acted— He paused, not wanting to complete the thought. But only one word suited her manner. Strange. That he'd even had such a thought annoyed him. She wasn't strange or different, not in the way people claimed. She was an individualist. He saw nothing peculiar in that. But today, right now, he mused, something was different about her. Silently cursing himself, he pushed the thought aside and grabbed the check that the waitress had slapped on the table. "If you're ready, let's go."

Jillian followed him to the cash register. Once more, she glanced back at the wheel. Could she have been wrong? she wondered. The thought hung in her mind as they stepped outside.

"We could go home if you're not feeling well—" David started to say.

Jillian fought her own troubled thoughts. "I want to keep looking for someone who—" She cut her words short. The droning of an engine suddenly sounded like a roar as a semitruck zipped into the parking lot next to the restaurant. Stunned, Jillian watched the truck fishtail. Without enough pause for her to catch her breath, the trailer jerked away from the cab and then hit the wall of the restaurant with a thump that resounded in the air. Beneath the impact, the building shuddered.

Through the restaurant window, she watched the wheel jump from the wall. She heard screams, but her eyes were riveted to the wheel spinning across the middle of the room. It rammed several chairs in its path before stopping at the other end of the restaurant. Each breath she drew ached as she visually scanned the shattered tables and chairs for a sight of the child. Frightened, her eyes wide and tearful, the little girl had buried herself in her mother's lap. Inches from the child was the broken wheel.

"Too close," David murmured then looked at her. "That was too close for—" The rest of his words remained unsaid. He saw panic in her face. It surprised him. She'd always given the impression of being steady during a crisis. But her hands were clenched to the straps of her shoulder bag, and her face was pale. "No one's hurt," he assured her, slipping an arm around her shoulder.

Jillian jumped at his touch. Steeling emotions never was easy. Her nerves were strung tight. A weakness flooded her, but self-preservation was stronger. Just as she concealed her clairvoyance, she'd always schooled herself to hide the turmoil that unsteadied her in the aftermath of a vision. "No. No one was hurt," she said softly more to herself than him.

David noted the color returning to her face. Looking for something to lighten the moment, he added on a mirthless laugh, "But that truck driver needs lessons on parking his semi."

For the first time in an hour, she felt normalcy slipping over her. That he hadn't seemed to question her reactions as odd relaxed her. But a quivery sensation made her limbs feel weak. Testingly she took a step toward his Jeep. "Where do we go now?"

"Good question," he answered. It was one of a dozen questions in his mind. He asked none of them. During the drive out of town, he realized how outrageous some of them were.

"Fifteen miles to the next real town," Jillian told him when he turned at the junction. She ran her finger along the highway line on the map. "Or Jacobsville is five miles away."

David roused himself from his own puzzled thoughts. "Too small. One gas station. One general store. Same building."

"Let's try it."

He slanted a glance at her. "Woman's intuition?"

"Something like that," she answered.

The woman behind the cash register wore a perpetual scowl. She listened to David's explanation, nodded her head and popped a chocolate bonbon into her mouth. "I don't know a lot about the hubby's business," she mumbled. "He says that I run my house, and he runs the garage. That's fine with me," she quipped before popping in another chocolate.

"Is he around?"

Looking like a chipmunk, she shook her head. "No. Would I be standing behind this cash register if he was?" she managed between chews. "Oh, I can be counted on to help run this place when he wants to take off and go fishing."

"When will your husband be back?" Jillian asked.

"Do you know my husband?"

Aware of the woman's jealous scrutiny of Jillian, David jumped in. "My client is in the same kind of business as your husband is. He regularly bought auto parts from one man, a traveling salesman."

She stared dumbly at him. "So?"

"Did your husband have a regular distributor?"

She scanned her surroundings disgustedly. "This isn't exactly a thriving business. He bought from different salesmen. But I don't know their names." Squinting, she focused on the box of chocolates. "One of them, I'd tar and feather if I ever saw him again. Do you know what he did to my Clyde? Well, I'll tell you what he did," she went on without taking a breath. "Clyde explains uppitylike to me, that the salesman can sell cheaper because he sells in bulk. That's when Clyde informed me that he'd bought more than he needed to. Dang fool."

"Why—" Jillian started. David squeezed her hand, silencing her.

"Some men don't have no common sense, do they? I knew something wasn't right. Clyde learned I was right. He was talking to a friend over in Beaver. My Clyde isn't really a dumb man," she added as an afterthought. "So when he sees that Arnie, the friend in Beaver, has boxes of car distributors by the same manufacturer that Clyde had, he mentions this salesman. Arnie says the salesman isn't in business anymore and took his money for another shipment, but never delivered the goods. Clyde was fit to be tied. Before the evening was over I had a living room full of crates and unpacked gaskets, spark plugs and lifters. Grumbling and swearing, Clyde tears out of the house. A couple of hours later, he comes back so mad that I thought he'd bust."

"What did he tell you?" David asked.

"When he was at Arnie's, he saw a magazine article about a heist. Someone swiped all kinds of automobile parts from a semi. I shrugged, not knowing why Clyde was so mad. Then he tells me. He's real good with numbers." She made a face. "As a matter of fact, he's got a memory an elephant would love. He's reading the article and sees some serial numbers of the stolen parts. He was sure that he had them. Sure enough, he did."

"And this man sold them to him?"

"I told Clyde then that you don't get anything for nothing." She raised her chin a notch. "I always thought something funny was going on. Otherwise, why was he selling them at such a discount? But Clyde sometimes thinks he knows it all."

David handed her his card. "When your husband comes back, I'd appreciate it if you'd have him call me."

The woman stared at the business card while picking up another chocolate. She answered with a nod, her cheeks puffed again.

"Jackpot," David said as they strolled toward the Jeep.

"Do you think he's the right one?"

"We can only hope." He opened the Jeep door for her. "In a few days, I'll check back with Clyde Vale, and get the man's name from him."

She nodded. "Why did you squeeze my hand?"

"If you'd led her too much, we'd have trouble. We might need her testimony. It has to be freely given. I don't want the prosecutor discrediting her story." He flicked on the ignition. "I would have skipped this place if you hadn't insisted."

Tension rippled and tightened the muscles in her shoulders for a second before she realized that she was making more out of his comment than necessary. "I always thought that I'd be great in Las Vegas."

He stared at her for a long moment then shifted into drive. She had a knack for guessing. Nothing more, David told himself. "We should celebrate," he said as he made the final turn toward Lakeside.

"Celebrate?"

"Someplace nice for dinner."

She slanted a look at him. "Are you asking me to have dinner with you?"

"Isn't that what I said?"

"In a roundabout way."

"We can stop at the Lakeside View Restaurant."

Jillian frowned and glanced down at her clothes. "I'm not dressed—"

"Properly?"

She laughed at his disbelieving tone. "I occasionally consider what's proper and what isn't."

Amusement sparkled in his eyes. "It's a weeknight. They only go there dressed to the nines on weekends."

"Okay, but I bet we still get stares."

He smiled at her. She'd always get stares. She stirred excitement. She walked into a room and made a man wonder if he was man enough for her. She'd gotten under his skin, hadn't she?

People stared. Jillian knew they would. But their interest wasn't focused on her clothes or his jeans. As they trailed the hostess to a table near the wall of windows, whispers followed David and her.

Jillian stared out at the moonlight shimmering on the lake. Without glancing around the restaurant, she guessed people were gossiping about them. Why was David Logan, the town's most prominent lawyer, having dinner with the spacey Mulvane from Raven Lane? A hex on all of them, Jillian thought with a sigh. She planned on enjoying the evening. "You lied, David." She hunched forward to whisper across the candlelit table. "They do dress to the nines during the week."

"Even in that outfit, you're the most beautiful woman here."

She laughed because she was unprepared for the compliment. He didn't toss them around freely. He was a controlled man, cautious. "I hope you won't regret that you brought me here."

His thumb stroked the top of her hand. "If I regret anything, it's that I didn't see the woman beneath Madam Jilliana before this."

"Ah, you have an extra sense now."

"No sense, until now, it would seem."

She toyed with the thin stem of her wineglass. "You're much too hard on yourself, counselor. There was no reason for us to be anything but passing acquaintances. If it weren't for Andy's predicament now, you and I would never—"

"Cut it out," he said softly.

She knew some men who raised their voices and had less effect.

"This has nothing to do with Andy. Don't pretend it does."

"No, it doesn't." As the warmth of his hand penetrated hers, an acceptance slithered over her. So did fear. Things needed to be said first. She'd promised herself years ago that she'd never let fate determine the course of her heart again. Years ago, she'd foolishly allowed herself to believe that if a man cared for her and loved her that he'd accept her as she was. She knew differently now. Logic, she mused. David would laugh if he knew that she was struggling for it at this moment when they sat close, his hand on hers, candlelight dancing across their faces.

He watched her gaze sweep the room. "Don't worry about them. When I was younger, I made a vow to make people regret the way that they treated my family so one day I wouldn't care what they thought."

Her eyes shifted back to meet his. "And you've done that."

"I wish I had." A sadness crept into his voice. "My mother died right before I finished law school. She never escaped the whispers. And when I came back here, money was tight at first. I was a new lawyer. Clients weren't flocking to my door. So I worked at night in the lumber mill."

"I never knew that."

"I still had a family to support. By then, Carolyn was living in Madison and had her nursing degree. She'd send money home to help out."

"It wasn't easy."

"No, it wasn't. But eventually I got what I wanted. I'm a member of Agnes's elite group, I've sat through dinner with the governor, and I have enough clients to keep me busy and solvent."

"What did you have to give up for all that?"

His head snapped up. "What?"

"Anytime you get everything you think you want, you have to give up something. Sometimes what you give up is worth losing for what you gained. Sometimes it isn't."

Her thought-provoking words came close to the truth. He'd given up the freedom to do what he wanted for the sake of respect and reputation. But he'd set high standards because his father had had such amoral ones. Had the rigidness of his life-style been worth it? He'd thought so. He'd never questioned it before. Until now. David touched the rim of his coffee cup. Why would she make such a comment? What had she given up? he wondered. "After high school, what did you do?"

"I worked in Mama's shop and attended college in Whitewater."

"Studying...?"

Staring down, she swirled the wine in her glass. "Astronomy. Later, I went to Tucson."

David grinned over the rim of the wineglass at her. "So why didn't you go into that field?"

"I knew about cosmos and quarks and sunspots. Mama was very thorough in her education of the world beyond. And to sit and stare through a telescope day after day for the rest of my life with the hopes of finding some new star or galaxy that could be named after me seemed like a boring way to spend my life."

"You might have liked it."

"I tried it for a while in Tucson. I spent hours at Kitt Observatory. I never found anything interesting there," she said in a suddenly sad tone.

Observing people went along with his profession. He had to gauge the honesty in a client's words. Though she was speaking truth to him, he sensed that she was leaving something unsaid. "No new star?"

"No. I fell off a cloud, though," she admitted.

David held his coffee cup in midair. "Love?"

She smiled wide. "You are very good at reading between the lines."

"I'm trained, too. Did it end sadly?"

"It ended. Anytime something that touches your heart ends, it leaves you sad."

"And you couldn't forecast such an ending by looking into your crystal ball?"

"I see the cynic is still with me this evening." She stared at the rose liquid in her glass. "I'd fallen in love and didn't want to feel beyond the happiness I had at that moment. What happened between Jason and me was predictable—expected."

"Why was that?"

"He was too different from me. He was studying physics. He believed science controlled everything." An amused smile suddenly turned up her lips. "Even love. He believed my scent drew us together."

David matched her grin. How often had the scent of lilacs haunted him recently? "There's supposed to be some truth to that."

"I could accept the concept of attraction existing because of a chemistry between us. But everything had to be proven to him."

"His analytical mind turned you off?"

"No, my mystical one confused him." She took a sip of wine and contemplated how much to tell him. "He tried to analyze me," she finally said. "He believed that I was living in a fantasy world because I was afraid of reality. Do you?"

His brows bunched with his frown. "We're the product of our upbringings."

"Oh, David, not always," she said softly. "You aren't."

"Of course I am."

"No, you aren't. If you hadn't been such an honest man who cared so much about his family name and about respect, you'd never have felt so compelled to undo the harm that your father had done. You'd have sloughed it off and left this town, never looking back. But you stayed. You took over the responsibilities of helping to raise your brother and sister. That had nothing to do with your father. The goodness within you made you react that way."

"Goodness?" His mouth twisted in an ironic grin. "When I look at you then, is the devil making me think what I'm thinking?"

"Are you having evil thoughts?"

"Wonderful ones."

"Hormones," she quipped, parroting his own response during an earlier conversation.

He chuckled. "Who's shying away from romance now?"

She raised her eyes. "Romance?"

Reaching forward, he lifted the rose from the bud vase and clipped it off between his fingers. Staring at eyes that he could get lost in, a madness swept over him. He longed to take his fill of what so far he'd only tasted.

With a touch so light that she barely felt it, he tucked the flower in her hair above her ear. As heat warmed her blood, cowardliness crept over her. She knew at that moment that she wouldn't tell him about the visions. She wanted these moments, any moments she could have with him.

"Romance," he whispered against her cheek.

Chapter Seven

"When I said romance last night this wasn't what I had in mind," David said between huffs as he pumped the bike up a hill.

"Out of shape, counselor?" Jillian jibed with a glance over her shoulder at him.

"Enough's enough. I haven't ridden a bike this much since I had a paper route."

"We'll stop over the hill."

"What's over the hill? A first-aid station?"

"A meadow of flowers. Blue forget-me-nots."

He wasn't used to wasting time, he reflected while pushing down the kickstand seconds later. The women he'd known had been career oriented. He'd attended mostly social functions with them, where they could meet the right people. With any other woman, he'd have resisted sitting under a willow, leaning back against the trunk and relaxing while she picked flowers. With Jillian, everything seemed right.

He watched her wandering through the meadow, stopping, inhaling the flowers' fragrance. But as peaceful as the surroundings were, he felt edgy, restless. She was responsible for that, too. He wanted her. He understood his own physical needs. He was too old not to. What he didn't understand was the compelling need just to hear her voice, make her smile, watch her. No other woman had ever done that to him, he realized while he visually followed her path through the meadow. Bending down for more flowers, she tossed back her hair. Beneath the sunlight, it appeared copper.

"Pretty flowers," she said, holding them close to her nose while she strolled toward him. Jillian had never expected real romance. It was something that love songs and movies offered; it was fantasy. Yet as he held her with a look, a moment of truth was closing in on her. She watched desire darken his eyes and felt an avalanche of emotions, beyond something as simple as longing. He could soften her with a smile. He could make her forget all the years when she'd been snubbed by too many people.

"Do you like flowers?"

She smiled at his reminder of the yellow rose, of the flowers that he'd sent her at nine that morning. A lush bouquet of tropical orchids had arrived in a tall vase shaped like a sitting cat.

"He had my mother call half a dozen florists as far as Oshkosh for this vase," the delivery boy had told her.

At that moment Jillian had merely nodded, too stunned to offer more response. David stirred conflicting feelings in her. And while her head screamed for self-preservation, her heart cried out for love. Her heart was definitely winning, she mused. "You know that I do," she answered. "Isn't that why you sent the orchids this morning?"

Grabbing her hand, he tugged her down beside him. "You like exotic things," he said softly while his fingertip traced a dimple in her cheek. "I like lilacs." He shifted her into the crook of his arm, wanting to drown in the scent of only one fragrance—hers. "They remind me of you."

The tip of his tongue enticed her. Little more was needed. She sighed and then closed her eyes, letting her other senses absorb the moment. The scent of flowers floated on a gentle breeze. The chirp of birds, the scurrying of a squirrel, the rustle of leaves blended together. As he angled her closer, his hand moving down her hip, she felt more than the warmth of desire moving through her. She was falling in love with him. At what moment had it started? Where could it take them? she wondered. Breathless from his kiss, she rested her cheek against his, wanting the impossible to be possible.

By the time they returned to town, the moon was hiding behind a cloud as if seeking shelter from an oncoming storm. Jillian had noted David's Jeep parked at the corner service station. Days had passed since she'd offered that warning. Instinctively her stomach quivered as if butterflies had taken flight.

"Let's walk the bikes up the hill," David suggested.

Jillian snapped herself back to her surroundings. "Tired?"

David eyed the incline to her house. "My legs could handle it, but not my backside."

"Soft," Jillian jibed, but the giggle in her throat never slipped out. Inwardly she tensed at Lillian Hilden's approach. "Good evening, Mrs. Hilden."

The woman passed them without even a nod.

Curiosity made Jillian glance back. Though Lillian was walking forward, her head was swiveled so far around as she stared after them that she should have unhinged it. "Do you know what Lillian is going to do?"

"She's going to rush to the closest phone and call her bosom buddy."

"Agnes is going to be on your doorstep at dawn. Probably with a lynch party."

"What's my crime?"

"Fraternizing with Jillian Mulvane."

"If you're right, I'm going to have an interesting day tomorrow."

Jillian tilted her head. "David, is something wrong with you?"

He chuckled. "No. Why would you think that?"

"You're acting funny."

He bent his head and kissed her.

It was a quick kiss, yet long enough to catch the attention of several people on the street. He was tempting fate. **Though she firmly believed that some things were predestined, she doubted if he was prepared for** what fueling gossip might do to his career. "You do want to go on practicing law in Lakeside, don't you?"

Stepping to the side, he moved her with his hip to avoid a pothole in the road.

Jillian didn't miss his devil-may-care grin. "You'd better act more cautious."

"We're reversing roles tonight, aren't we?" he asked while he leaned his bike against the banister of her house.

Jillian dug into her jeans pocket for the keys and climbed the steps. "We're wrong for—"

David stood beside her at the door. "Everything is right," he whispered.

Their faces were close. His eyes met hers with a soft understanding look that was more unsettling than one filled with desire. "Being twitter pated might be dangerous," Jillian warned.

"I'll take that chance," he said softly against her cheek before pushing open the door and urging her inside.

She shivered beneath the sensuous trace of his fingertips down the curve of her neck. "David—"

"Ssh," he whispered and shut the door with his foot.

As if she were under a spell, she followed the command of the hand cupping the back of her neck, drawing her closer. She yearned for the tenderness that she wanted to resist. She ached for the demanding pressure she felt in the warm, firm mouth moving over hers. She needed the reality that this man forced into her life. She'd pretended too long that she could stay detached and blissful in a world she'd made safe by avoiding such moments with any man. But he wasn't any man. For him, she was weak. For him, she would let herself do the one thing she'd struggled to avoid. She would give her heart, she realized, as she followed him into the bedroom.

When he lowered her to the bed, she clung to him, answering his kiss, absorbing his taste, wanting more. She doubted that she'd have ever pulled away from him willingly. Because she needed him, she didn't want to think about tomorrow. Tonight. Only tonight was important.

As Jillian's arms tightened around his neck, David buried a hand in the mass of red curls and felt the strands entwining around his fingers. He twisted his mouth across hers. He knew he was bruising her lips yet couldn't seem to satisfy the craving for her taste. Sweet. Intoxicating, it was like a sorcerer's potion.

She wasn't what he'd thought. She was fragile and sensitive yet more real than any woman he'd ever known. His life had always been so serious, filled with so many responsibilities. She was like a never-ending feeling of lightness. Even during serious moments, something about the warmth in her eyes eased him. For the first time in his life, he found himself wondering about fantasy. Wondering what was real and what wasn't. And then, he drew her tight to him again and he realized that nothing mattered but the feel of her softness against him.

He captured her breath in his mouth and ground his lips against hers one more time as if this were the last time he'd kiss her. But it wouldn't be the last. Never the last, David told himself as he skimmed the outline of her body with a hand.

For the first time in his life, he wanted to give pleasure as much as receive it. With every kiss she returned, with every fluttering caress of her hand, his blood pounded harder. As a frenzy began within him, she tugged at his shirt. It was all the urging he needed. Possessively his hands made quick work of her blouse and then tugged down her jeans. With a low moan, he nibbled at the thin silk still covering her. He'd hoped for gentleness, but he lost the control then. His mouth clinging to hers, he shoved aside the rest of their clothes. When she arched against him with the same pulsating need, he no longer could think much less reason.

Passion clawed at him. In the moonlit room, her skin was bathed by a silvery sheen. She was lovelier than he'd imagined. She was bewitching. She was the vision of every passionate dream he'd known. He'd been waiting for her all these years, and she'd always been so close. If a sensible thought existed in his mind, it couldn't find its way through the maze of sensations taking control over him.

He touched what he'd only allowed himself to imagine before this. He kissed her breast, then caught a nipple, letting his tongue roll over it until she arched again in response as if trying to blend her flesh with his. In his wildest imagination he hadn't conjured such softness. Then almost like a jolt to bring him back to reality, his pulse and heart began pounding. Desire curled around him, and muscles tightened with an aching that promised a pain too filled with pleasurable torment to battle.

She knew the moment that his mood changed. The steady hands roaming over her skin grew more demanding. The kisses became hungrier. She found herself gasping to keep pace with the madness. As his lips blazed a trail of small, passionate kisses from her breasts to her tummy then coursed a path lower, she felt a long, head-to-toe shudder moving through her. Beneath her hands, his skin grew damp with passion. His touch no longer soothed and stroked but insisted until she was writhing beneath the slightest brush of a finger. Breathless, she murmured his name over and over as she stroked his back, cupped his buttocks, caressed his inner thigh. She waited for the sound of his soft groan. She waited for the moment when they'd reached the edge of some precipice, when they'd cling together, when they'd finally tumble over.

Her soft sounds mingled in a song of surrender, then as if given new strength, she coiled her arms and legs around him in a viselike grip. He watched the wave of a shudder pass over her face, before he pressed himself down on her, before he plunged into her. Her eyes never left his as their flesh blended, as their bodies moved with a oneness that he thought impossible. He felt himself seeking the rainbows, the moon that only she seemed capable of making him want. He felt himself reaching for the stars overhead.

Her hands clung to him, journeying with him, urging him upward, rushing him to find something that he'd thought was impossible, a world where reality and fantasy melded. Then all thoughts stopped, and nothing mattered but the love they were sharing.

A noise stirred him, a soft thumping sound above him. David stared up at the dark ceiling, wondering with amusement if she had an oversize mouse in the attic. He glanced at the window to see the moon slip behind a cloud. For a long moment, he didn't move, unwilling to weave his way past the scent of lilacs, the warmth and the softness of the body that seemed to fit in perfect alignment with his as if they were two puzzle pieces made for each other. "I have a confession," he finally murmured against her collarbone.

"What?" she asked drowsily, unsure why she was questioning anything.

Tangled in the cover, he shifted. "About Agnes."

"Agnes?" A frown etched a faint line between her brows. "What about her?"

"I'm representing her."

Not opening her eyes, Jillian brushed her cheek across his. "I know you're her lawyer, David."

"I've been given a special assignment that involves you."

"To do what?"

David skimmed the round softness of her hip. "Get this house from you."

Jillian forced herself to pay attention. Pulling away, she raised her face and peered in the darkness at him. "How are you doing that?"

Not deterred, David bent his head toward her breast. "She had a suggestion."

As his breath warmed her flesh, she sighed. "A suggestion?"

His mouth hovered close to her nipple. "She suggested persuasion of a different kind."

"Ah," she said on another sigh. "That's what this is all about?"

"I can't plead guilty."

She nipped his ear. "You can't?"

He heard her smile. "Agnes has nothing to do with *this*."

Running a hand over the back of his head, she arched toward him. "Whatever your reason, I suggest that you give it your best try."

"I planned to." He paused, his tongue joining in the play. "Want to know why?"

As he braced himself over her and kissed her belly, Jillian hummed with sensation. "Yes," she answered softly.

"Because I'm crazy about you."

Her eyes closed. "Is that all?"

"Because I never wanted anything as much as I want you."

"David, I—" As the heat of his breath warmed her thigh, she curled her fingers around his shoulders. "I won't sell," she managed in a whispery laugh.

"I know," he murmured then lowered his head.

A hazy sunlight streamed through the lace curtain. Burying her face against his shoulder, Jillian touched his chest. His breathing was slow and steady. So different from last night. But then so much had changed in a few hours. What had she been afraid of? Why had she tormented herself? Tomorrow didn't matter. Only today. She clung to that thought. As he stirred, snuggling closer, she kissed his chest. "I bet you like an enormous breakfast."

"Coffee."

"Tea?"

His teeth found the delicate shell of her ear. "You," he mumbled.

"You're easy to please."

"Never. You've spoiled me."

Urged by the sudden quickening of his heart, she rolled and pressed down on him. Staring into his eyes, she grinned while she traced the faint curve bracketing his lips.

She looked young, impish. Last night, he'd felt as if he'd been with a woman wise beyond her years in the ways of love. "You gave me a love potion, didn't you?" he asked, brushing strands of hair away from her cheek.

"My never-fail one."

"Does it wear off?"

"I hope not."

He framed her face with his hands and drew it close. "Me, either." Because he treated nothing lightly, he needed more than the intimacy of flesh with her. No barriers, he mused, aware now of the delicate path he'd have to journey for such closeness with her.

As the change in his mood registered, she raised herself and stared into eyes. They were intense and searching.

"Don't let it," he appealed softly. "Talk to me. Trust me." He felt the stiffening in her back and shoulders and held firm, pressing both palms against the small of her back to keep her on top of him.

"I don't know what you're talking—"

"Jill—" He drew a hard breath to keep an impatient demand out of his voice. "Ask me about the Jeep."

She willed herself to stay calm. "It needed repair?"

"You told me it would."

For fear she'd give away her own anxiousness, she avoided his eyes. "Anything serious?"

"The steering column was ready to break."

A flutter of uneasiness skittered over her.

"You told me that I'd have mechanical trouble." At her troubled expression, David pressed his lips to her jaw. "How did you know?" he questioned softly.

Like a butterfly's caress, his mouth had grazed her flesh reassuringly. But nothing would help her at the moment, she realized. Curling her fingers around the sheet, she rolled away and pushed herself up. Only then, when his body no longer touched hers, did she meet his eyes. She saw questions. Doubts.

"Why? Why did you insist on sitting at that table in the restaurant?" He searched her eyes. Even as he'd asked the question, he was fighting the idea he was suspecting. He'd heard about parapsychology. He knew her mother claimed to have powers. But he was a doubter. Even now, despite the problem with the car and the incident in the restaurant, he wanted to believe her reactions were coincidences. But the woman he'd begun to know was more than an eccentric who lived in the Raven Lane house. David forced the words out. "The Stargazer is a cover-up, isn't it?"

Nakedness made a person vulnerable, Jillian mused. She'd had her back against a wall before this and worked her way out. "Cover-up?" she asked in a light tone that she hoped hid her nervousness.

"Cover-up," David insisted. He scooted to sit up beside her. "The store." Grabbing her shoulders, he forced her to face him. "The crystal ball, the whole zany, eccentric bit is a cover-up."

She placed a hand on his chest and pushed him away.

"It's a lot of mumbo jumbo to hide—" He hesitated, unsure what to call something he'd never given credence to before. "Psychic powers?"

There it was, Jillian thought. She could deny the truth in his words. But she'd only be hurt later when he rejected the idea as nonsense, when he stood before her as Jason had and scoffed that she was out of her mind. "Yes," she said softly, staring out the window. Outside a breeze swayed the limbs of an oak tree. One leaf fluttered from the security of the branch.

For a second, he stared at her naked back. It was slender and delicate looking. But the woman it belonged to wasn't. She was stronger than she looked, David realized. While he'd worried what other people thought of him, she'd deliberately allowed people to think less of her, not see her intelligence and sensitivity. To hide the truth, she'd presented them with an image they could accept. With his hand on her shoulder, he turned her around to face him. Eyes filled with sadness met his. In their cool blueness, he saw memories of kids taunting, the adults snickering whenever her mother passed by.

"My mother warned me to keep that to myself."

He held firm beneath her scrutinizing stare.

"Does it bother you?" she asked.

"I don't know what it means," he answered honestly.

"Clairvoyance."

"What's it like?"

His curiosity was expected, but she kept waiting for a ridiculing look to settle on his face. Working in the store, she watched the expression on faces when skepticism gave way to a more open-minded attitude. She'd learned to live with people thinking her an odd sort. But "the gift" she'd inherited from her mother was too personal. She knew how vulnerable she'd be if people knew. Psychics were considered weird or fakes. She could accept being thought of as eccentric. But the fear of being mocked about something she herself had had to learn to live with left her too vulnerable. And now he knew. Why had she thought that he wouldn't see through her act? Other people assumed she was lucky at guessing. Why hadn't he?

A silence hung in the air like a thick curtain. Long moments passed before he spoke. "When did this visionary ability begin?"

He was a man who needed proof, she realized. "A long time ago."

"As a child?"

She nodded.

"Did Carolyn know that?"

She wanted to run from the moment. Melancholy shadowed her, insisting that she remember one thing. No man would ever want to live day in and day out with a freak. Especially not David. He'd struggled too hard to gain acceptance to chance ever losing it. "Yes, your sister knew. Besides my family, she and Myra were the only ones who knew. My mother told me people hated what they didn't understand. I saw the ridicule she went through. I knew better than to make an announcement." He'd leave her alone now, she told herself. But even before she finished the thought, he curled an arm around her shoulder and drew her closer to him.

He tightened his hold instinctively as he felt her body tense. "Jill—"

He looked so troubled that Jillian wanted to ease his mind. "Now you understand."

"Understand what?"

"I saw my mother's pain, David. Her husbands didn't understand. They tried to, but they had difficulty accepting her business, her scrying, her forecasts. Her oddity," she added softly.

"There are a lot of things I don't understand," he said, frowning, "but I don't run from them."

"I can't change." She wished that she could reassure him, but she couldn't. "Jason couldn't understand or accept that."

"I'm not asking you to change," he said angrier than he'd intended as a twinge of hurt swept through him that she'd pigeonholed him with another man. He tangled a leg with hers, needing to touch more of her, wanting to protect her from what had already happened, yet knowing he couldn't change the past.

Almost as if needing a gauge, she placed her hand on his chest. His heart beat steadily, reassuringly. "It's not always pleasant," she tried to remind him, wishing she could warn him about the unexpected. But of course, she couldn't. He'd never truly understand until he experienced it, until he stood near and watched her go into a trance that took total control of her, until he felt the distance from her even though he stood near. "I can't call it up whenever I want to, and I can't make it go away because I want it to. Sometimes it's just there."

"Premonitions?"

"Yes." She responded to the hand that was insisting she rest her head on his chest. She doubted his calm acceptance. She wished that she didn't, but she'd seen every man who'd entered her mother's life offer token reassurances that they understood. None of them had. For the moment, she wanted to believe in David. She knew how to pretend, she reflected and listened to the strong beat of his heart. Wasn't his steadiness part of what appealed to her? He was like a rock. His sister, Carolyn, had teasingly referred to him that way. But now Jillian understood why. At this moment, he seemed stronger than anyone she'd ever known, he seemed willing to accept any part of her burden. When the moment of truth came, and it would, she reminded herself, she'd remember the times like this and cling to them for an eternity.

"Jill?"

"I didn't mean to tell you," she said softly. "I shouldn't have told you about the Jeep, but I didn't want to see you hurt."

Gently he stroked her hair. "And I don't want to hurt you."

If his tenderness hadn't weakened her, then his words would have. He'd said the exact words she'd needed to hear at that moment. A shiver of uncertainty—perhaps fear, she realized—rippled through her.

"Ever," he assured her before turning her chin up.

The gentleness of his lips on hers soothed. The caress of a tender hand gave her solace. She responded to his kiss, to his touch, to his sensitivity, to the eyes staring down at her. So clear and honest. She saw no disbelief, no uncertainty in them. She'd felt no hesitancy in his kiss. He knew now what she'd strived to hide for years. He knew and had still kissed her. He'd accepted her as she was.

For a little while, she'd believe in him, in what might never be possible. She shifted, curling her arms around his neck, and fastened her mouth on his. With no thought but of the moment, she touched him until reality slipped away, until she'd gathered strength from him. She gave him everything that she'd held back from all others, for he'd given her something no one else ever had. He'd accepted her. She knew it wasn't forever. She didn't expect this to be for more than the moment, however many they might have. She only knew that he was the one that she wanted it all with. All the pleasure, all the sensations, all the loving that was possible between two people.

Hands relentlessly moved over flesh. Lips followed now familiar paths. She moaned beneath the touch of his mouth as it sought every inch of her. She'd never felt such caring, such emotion for any man—from any man. He caressed and she felt weak. He kissed and breathed new strength into her. Over and over again, he stirred her with a stroke of his hand, the brush of his mouth, the gentle swipe of his tongue. Wild with need, aching from wants, she pushed him to a limit. As his hands tightly pressed into her flesh, she lowered herself to him. She felt a control on her life that she'd never known before. No one else had ever offered it to her before. She felt secure with it. She felt as if her world couldn't be shaken again. She told herself such false security was from the heat of the moment. But she didn't care. She took him into her with a greediness that tensed every muscle of her body.

She absorbed him until she felt the strength flowing from her, until she felt drained. Until she felt contentment.

Grudgingly David agreed to a breakfast of tea and rice cakes. He eyed what resembled cut-up sections of waffled doormats and sipped the tea slowly.

She moved around the kitchen with a fluid swiftness. She could move sensuously slow, too, he mused, remembering the night before. He'd felt like a teenager again despite years of experience. He'd felt the quick passion, the aching, the yearning for the unknown. Each time she'd made him want her more. Even now, desire seemed at the brink of breaking loose.

"Does Agnes really want this house?" she asked while rifling through the contents of the refrigerator for jelly.

"I'm supposed to make you an offer that you won't refuse."

"But you never did."

"I thought I'd have been wasting my breath."

"You would have been. I won't sell."

"Let me give you a warning this time. Agnes can be persuasive." He ran his fingers across his unshaven jaw. "You know, you've told me why you won't sell it. What I can't figure out is why Agnes is so determined all of a sudden to have this house."

"She wants to make staying in Lakeside difficult for me."

David frowned. "We'll fight her."

She drew a hard breath. For so long, she'd felt as if she were standing alone. Frozen to the spot, she searched his face. "You'll help?"

He pushed himself to a stand and strode toward her. With his hands, he framed her face. "You have to ask that?"

"Oh, David." She leaned into him. "You offer so much."

"You give so much." A wry grin curled the edges of his lips as he glanced back at the plate on the table. "Except for breakfast," he teased.

Sliding her arms around his waist, she smiled. "You don't like the rice cakes?"

David grimaced at the bland-looking cakes. "No, but you have such fine other attributes."

"Do I?"

He skimmed his lips over the shell of her ear. "Many."

From downstairs, a buzzer drifted up the stairway.

He feigned a disappointed tone. "Guess I'll have to forget the breakfast."

"Saved by the bell," she said lightly.

Nuzzling her neck, he urged, "Or we could forget both."

Jillian danced away from him. "Someone is at the store entrance. I have to answer it."

He sidled close again. "No, you don't."

"Yes, I do." She pushed a hand against his chest and slipped from his embrace. "Anticipation is supposed to be the true titilation," she said with a laugh.

"Rubbish," he returned and received another giggle as an answer. David snatched up his windbreaker and joined her on the landing. Bent forward, she was looking over the banister to see through the semicircular, etched-glass window at the top of the door.

"Cornelia Quinton and Iris Ogilvy," she informed him.

From his loftier vantage point, David saw the crown of Cornelia's head bobbing as she chattered away. He smiled with a memory at the sight of the woman who'd taught him seventh grade. "Is Cornelia a regular customer of yours?"

"Yes." Jillian let her hand ride the banister as they descended the stairs. "After her husband died, she started coming here. He told her that he didn't believe in magic shops, so she never came before that. But she and Iris are regulars now. So I have to let them in." She shot a grin at him. "Want to duck out the back?"

He took a swipe at her backside.

With a giggle, Jillian dodged him, but she saw his frown. "They won't tell anyone that they saw you here this morning."

"That's not what worries me." He made a boyish face. "Knowing Cornelia, she'll feel compelled to reminisce about my youth."

Jillian took a step back to stand at eye level with him. "You don't like her?"

"I like her," he said honestly. During a difficult time in his life, after his father had left, she'd offered friendly advice—what people think isn't nearly as important as what we think. "But I wasn't one of her easiest students," he admitted.

Curling an arm around his neck, Jillian leaned into him. "I'll protect you," she teased.

"With some magic potion?"

"Only the kind that works on bright sunny days."

David glanced out the window. Heavy gray clouds threatened rain. "Jill, it isn't sunny."

"To me, it is," she said with another quick kiss before breezily hurrying toward the door.

Me, too, he realized. Sunshine had entered his life.

Chapter Eight

Oh, my. For such a gloomy day, I feel a bright aura surrounding me." With a discreet glance at David, Iris sighed and then resumed staring out one of the long narrow windows in the Stargazer.

David stifled a grin while he turned an amethyst over in his hand.

"For a change, I'm channeling in on your vibrations," Cornelia said, patting her friend's fleshy shoulder.

"When I awoke, I wasn't feeling so sunny." Iris stared at David while speaking to Cornelia. "I'm worried my daughter and son-in-law are headed for a divorce," she explained to him even though he hadn't asked a question. "I need a talisman that's guaranteed to put the spark back in their marriage." She stepped around Cornelia and sidled close to David.

"We're not supposed to be here," Iris whispered. "Riley closed the shop, you know."

"Agnes closed it," Cornelia countered. "Riley can't walk a straight line without his cousin's help."

Iris nodded agreeably. "But I called Jillian yesterday morning," Iris went on conspiratorially low to David. "This is the day of my regular reading. I never miss a week."

Cornelia lifted her chin slightly. "So we came anyway."

"Yes, Jillian said that it wouldn't get her in trouble."

David wasn't so sure of that.

"What can Riley or Agnes do?" Cornelia looked at Iris. "Friends have a right to visit a friend, don't they?"

"They do indeed, Cornie." Iris flashed a speculative smile at David. "I didn't know you were such a close friend of Jillian's, David." She gave a nod of approval to her friend. "Isn't that interesting?"

"Oh, my, yes."

Both women beamed at him.

As Jillian hurried down the steps from the loft, they whirled away from him.

"Did you find it?" Iris asked, rushing toward her.

"Yes, I did." Jillian held an amulet in the air before her.

"Oh, good. This is exactly what I need."

Cornelia nudged her. "For your son-in-law?"

"Jillian suggested it," Iris told her. "She said that I should drop the amulet in the breast pocket of Todd's suit."

"But he's a carpenter."

"Oh, Cornie, sometimes, you are so—" She stopped her criticism abruptly. "I offered to baby-sit tonight. I told them to go out and have a nice dinner on me at the Lakeside View Restaurant. A romantic evening." She winked. "The amulet guarantees that." She swung a look at Jillian again. "Doesn't it?"

"It's an amulet for lovers."

As she smiled at the women, David realized how much some people relied on her, not for hocus-pocus, but to brighten their day, to give them hope.

"And before they leave, I plan on making them a drink with lilacs in it."

David caught Jillian's eye.

"A white lilac with five instead of four petals is called the 'luck lilac,'" Jillian explained. "If it's swallowed easily then love is true."

"Otherwise, call the paramedics?" he quipped low.

Jillian sent him an indulgent smile.

Cornelia rolled her eyes. "David, David," she said in an exasperated tone. "You always were the stubbornest student I ever taught. I would tell the class something, and you'd challenge me to prove it. I see you haven't changed."

"Seventh grade was memorable, Mrs. Quinton."

"For me, too. But you must bend a little. Look at me. I've become quite proficient in doing astrological charts. I even did Jillian's."

"And what did you learn about her?" he asked with devilment in his eyes that Jillian had never noticed before.

"Because she's an Aquarian, she's stable but hates restrictions. She loves a sense of freedom. Her biggest fault is that she sees the world as she wishes it would be.''

"She's leaving out the good part," Jillian said lightly. "Aquarians are often nuisances."

"Not at all, dear. You care about other people." She looked back at David. "There's much more. But perhaps, you have your own way of learning all that," she teased. "You were never the one to follow what others did, David."

"If I gave you a difficult time years ago, I apologize."

"No need," Cornelia said with a wave of her hand. "I enjoyed every moment. Now I must go. Iris, are you ready?"

"Oh, yes. Don't you want to get an amulet like this for Albert?"

Cornelia linked her arm with her friend's and ushered her toward the door. "I don't need it anymore."

"Ooh," Iris cooed.

They walked out, giggling like schoolgirls.

"If only every person I know was like those two," Jillian said wistfully. "They are so sweet."

"Unlike your next-door neighbor and her good friend."

"Lillian isn't bad."

As she passed by him, he caught her hand and tugged her close. "That's gracious."

"She really isn't. Lillian isn't the one out to rid this town of Mulvanes. I know Agnes nudged her to complain about the Stargazer. Agnes is stronger, and Lillian bends. But she didn't always, at least not so much."

David rested his hands on the points of her hips.

"When I was little and her husband was still alive, they used to invite me in for cookies and milk." She smiled with a warm memory. "Actually her husband did. He was such a nice man. A happy person. He looked like Santa 'Claus. I miss him." She looked out the window toward Lillian's house then spun around as the phone rang. "I imagine that she does, too," she said, rushing to pick up the phone. "Stargazer."

"Jill, bad news."

She cupped a hand over the receiver and spoke to David, "I'll be a minute."

He nodded and strolled toward the display counter.

"Hi, Carol, is it about—"

"We don't have that building anymore."

Jillian felt her spirits droop. "It's gone? Already? I was going to look at the building at lunchtime. This is the second time. What happened?"

"Same as before. I called you as soon as I heard that Mr. Higgins was renting out the shop vacated by the blintz makers. But someone else signed a lease as I was talking to you."

"Who?"

"The city council leased it for use as a library branch."

"Why would they want to put a library branch there? It's in the middle of craft shops."

"I know. Sounds fishy to me, too. Especially after they pulled a similar stunt a few days ago. I'll keep looking, Jill."

"Thanks."

David moved closer.

"The building I was considering for my shop was leased out this morning," she informed him, offering a weak smile while setting the receiver back in its cradle.

"I overheard. To the library?"

"Yes."

"You said that was the second time?"

"Two days ago, Carol found another building for me. It would have been close to perfect. It was at the edge of town near the lake and the motels."

"What happened with that one?"

"I arrived to lease it just as Mayor Doyles was leaving. He said that the town council had been discussing a parking lot for boat trailers."

David nodded. "That's right. But no site had been picked."

"Guess you missed that meeting."

He looked away with a curse. "I think that you're being blocked."

"Agnes?"

In amazement David watched her lips curve in a smile.

"She really is going all out on her campaign to rid the town of witches, isn't she?"

Instinctively his arms tightened around her.

At the concern she saw in his eyes, she assured him, "I'm teasing. I'll find a place. She can only use the town council so much. Something will become available. It's karma," she added lightly.

"It's...?"

"Fate."

A month ago he'd have openly scoffed at her comment. That was a month ago, he mused. His vision wasn't so narrow anymore. She'd made him see things that he'd never imagined before. But still doubts remained. He couldn't get rid of them. He'd lived too much of his life questioning and expecting explanations to accept everything she seemed to believe in. "What about the amulet that you gave Iris? Will it be fate if the woman's daughter and son-in-law patch things up?"

"With a little help from friends."

"What did you give Iris?"

"An almond and three specks of rice in a locket. It represents an old Swedish superstition. When a bridegroom finds an almond in his rice pudding at the wedding, then the marriage is destined for happiness. That's why I gave her that one."

"Gave?"

"My shop is closed. Remember?" she asked, turning her back on him. "What her daughter and her husband really needed was time alone."

"So you suggested that Iris baby-sit?"

"Good common sense was called for this time."

David grinned. "You know about common sense."

"It's overrated," she said as he caressed her slender back.

People might be fooled by her. He wasn't anymore. She was resilient, strong. Capable. She was also vulnerable. "Do you need help with the packing?" he asked.

"Are you volunteering?"

As her weight fell against him, he chuckled. "For anything you want."

Jillian laid a hand on his chest and toyed with a button on his shirt. "Could I take a rain check?" he asked.

"For packing boxes?"

"For whatever you suggest."

She loved him, she realized. She couldn't think of any solution to what she felt for him that wouldn't cause heartache in time. So she took the most logical approach. She'd spend time with him, share with him, love him. And when the time came for the end, she'd accept the hurt. It would be worth it for the time that they did have together. "You have to go to the office, don't you?"

Her lips brushed lightly across his. He wondered if two people so opposite could make a life together. Could they learn to live with each other's idiosyncrasies? "Afraid so." He took one last, long taste of her mouth before heading toward the door. But he wanted to stay. He couldn't ever remember any woman coming first in his mind before work. With a glance back over his shoulder, he reminded her, "Rain checks are good forever."

A drizzle began at ten that morning. By dusk, raindrops plopped in a steady synchopated beat on the sidewalk outside David's office.

When he dug out Clyde Vale's phone number a half hour later, the storm had intensified. A sheet of rain obscured his view of the buildings across the street.

"Clyde ain't home yet," the man's wife informed him. "He'll be here soon, though."

"I thought that he might have cut his trip short." At the rumble of thunder, David glanced toward the window. "It's pouring out."

"Oh, that doesn't bother Clyde. He's like a duck," she mumbled, and David imagined that she'd popped another chocolate into her mouth between breaths.

"If you don't mind, I'll call him tomorrow then," he said.

"Fine and dandy," she mumbled back at him.

David set the receiver back in its cradle. His defense for Andy was stalled. After lunch, he'd gone to the county recorder's office. He'd found the parcel number and the name of the owner for the Pizza Palace restaurant in Farleyville. The man lived in Milwaukee and had an unlisted phone number. Tomorrow, David would have to pull strings to get it. Tonight, he needed fins to swim home. He watched lightning streak across the dark sky.

As a child, his sister, Carolyn, had hated storms. Most women hated them, he reflected, grabbing his windbreaker from his office closet. For that matter, he wasn't too fond of them himself.

Five minutes later, he was swearing savagely as the tires of his Jeep slid on the slick road. He slowed the Jeep to a snail's pace and peered out the window. The windshield wipers ineffectually swished against a slashing rain. A flash of lightning illuminated the roof of Jillian's house. David stared at the stalking figure on the roof. Something small and yellow.

Though he was cautious with his turn onto the driveway, the tires bounced over a rut and the rear of the Jeep slid sideways. David gripped the steering wheel while he blinked, thinking he was imagining what he was seeing. He caught himself gaping before he brought the Jeep to a stop. Wearing a yellow slicker with a hood, Jillian looked like a miniature version of Big Bird as she crawled across the top of the roof. Threateningly, a flash of lightning cracked across the sky again.

His heart thundered in his chest as he grabbed a flashlight from his glove compartment and then rushed from the Jeep. The wind howled. Almost punishingly, it whipped rain at his face during his dash to the side of the house. Beneath his feet, the ground was soft and slippery. One foot slid sideways in his haste before he reached the ladder. Blinking rain from his eyes, on an oath, David took his life in his hands and began climbing.

Jillian heard a creaking behind her. Though not skittish by nature, she gripped her flashlight, and then swung around, ready to land a blow if need be.

A shadowed head ducked before a familiar voice yelled out an earthy response. "It's me, dammit."

She peered through the sheet of rain. His hair was plastered to his scalp. "David?"

"Who the hell else would be up here with you?" he yelled over the crack of thunder. "Get down. Now," he ordered.

"I had a roof to fix."

Lightning flashed again, illuminating his face in an eerie glow. She saw a fury that was fiercer than the electrifying display overhead.

"You're getting down now."

"I'm done now," she yelled back at him.

He wiped a hand across his wet face as if to clear his vision. "It's fixed?"

"Yes."

"Then, let's get off this damn roof before one of us gets killed."

Jillian tramped past him, muttering, "You have a definite tendency toward exaggerating. No one is going to get killed."

"You may," he declared behind her.

She stopped at the edge of the roof and looked back at him.

"I'm very close to contemplating murder," he said.

For some reason, she felt like smiling as she carefully climbed down the ladder.

The inside of the house looked different. With the darkness, shadows seemed to dance on the wall. David felt edgy, something he'd admit to no one. Out of the corner of his eye, he kept noticing disturbing sights: the sway of a curtain, the damn cat stalking around almost nervously, the lurking image of a statue.

Outside the wind howled, whistling through the old house, banging shutters and wiggling doors. And through it all, Jillian moved with a relaxed gait as if the stormy night suited her more than a quiet, sunny day would. Though she flicked on a light switch, the room remained dark. "No power, no phone, nothing." She reached into a drawer of the hallway table for a candle and matches.

He heard the striking of the match. When he turned around, she was holding the candle at chin level. Light radiated on her face. "Why have you come to my house?" she said in a menacingly soft voice.

"Full of mischief, aren't you?" Threateningly he leaned his wet face closer to hers. Her eyes looked haunting, captivating. "To strangle your lovely neck, my dear." Though she whirled away, in the quiet darkness, he heard her soft laugh. "That wasn't meant to be funny. You could have done a real number on yourself up on that roof," he added in a tone that was filled more with concern than anger.

"I know," she returned and then disappeared into the kitchen.

David followed. "What if you'd fallen?" he asked as he glanced and sniffed at the pots on the stove. Whatever she'd been cooking had gone bad.

"Couldn't."

"Why not?"

"I had my broom." She tossed him a towel. "You're all wet."

He heard the airy lightness in her voice. She was finding the situation enjoyable. Any other woman would have been complaining about her roof leaking. Not her. "Would you like some tea?"

David whipped off his wet windbreaker. "Coffee."

"Instant?"

He grimaced. "If I have to. But you have no electricity."

"I have a sterno can. We could heat the water over that."

"I'll pass."

David sniffed again. Something smelled dead. "Were you cooking dinner?" he asked, noting the pots on the stove.

"Poultices. I sell them for leg ulcers, bee stings, rashes, and—" Even in the dark room, she could see his disbelieving expression. "Indian remedies," she assured him, suddenly aware of a thumping overhead. "Before the great witch doctor arrived on the scene, they had to find some way to heal. Nature provides a lot healthier ways than drugs."

"If they work."

"They work. In fact, one salve on the market is based on—" She cut her words short as he swiveled his head around and searched the darkness. "What's the matter?" she asked dumbly.

"What's the matter?" He swung a look of incredulity at her. "Didn't you hear that thumping?"

Jillian shrugged. "You're jumpy tonight."

"I'm not jumpy."

"Don't you like storms?"

He ignored her question and stilled in response to the banging. "There it is again."

"What is?"

In a searching manner, he slowly circled the kitchen. "Thumping."

"What thumping?"

"*That* thumping," he said with a jab of his hand toward the ceiling. The banging lasted a few seconds and then stopped again.

"That's nothing," Jillian said on a sigh, sensing only truth would end his concern. "Just Aunt Morgana."

David whipped around. "But she's—"

"Yes," Jillian said simply. "Aunt Morgana doesn't exactly live here." She avoided his scowl and set a lit candle in the center of the table. "Let's go into the living room."

His hand closed over hers on the table. "Are you—" He paused and narrowed his eyes at her. "Are you trying to tell me that—"

"She haunts this house."

His hand remained tight on hers. "That's just gossip."

"I suppose you'll need a full explanation before you'll believe me."

"I can't guarantee anything even then."

Jillian decided to ignore his jibe and pulled away to place lids on the pots of brewing liquid. "Grams—Aphrodite—"

"That was her name?"

She nodded without turning around. "Aphrodite had the ability to see through the crystal ball. One day, Aunt Morgana, my mother's sister, came home with Willard. He was her beau. Excitedly Aunt Morgana chattered on while she showed Grams the engagement ring that Willard had given her."

As David started to light another candle, Jillian shook her head. "There's no point in doing that. Aunt Morgana won't stand for it. Even one candle won't stay lit for long," she added.

David grinned at her indulgently. Having recovered from her announcement, he'd decided to humor her, sort of. "This is an old house, Jillian. The wind moves through it. That's why candles don't stay lit."

"Probably," she said agreeably.

Too agreeably, he reflected. But she couldn't possibly believe in ghosts. Settling back on the edge of the kitchen table, he assumed he was about to hear a ghost story befitting a stormy night. "Go on about Morgana."

"Well, Grams sat Morgana and Willard down and then stared into the crystal," Jillian continued. "Immediately she announced that he had no right to give Morgana the ring. It belonged to his wife."

David released a low whistle that turned her around. "Was he married?"

"Yes. And papa to three little ones. Later, Mama told me that Morgana learned his intentions weren't honorable. He'd given rings to several other women with the hope that such a symbol of his love would be adequate persuasion to get them into his bed."

"Scoundrel."

She nodded. "But you see Morgana was heartbroken."

"Why didn't she foresee this if she cast the runes?"

"You can't foresee for yourself usually. Only others. So she declared that she would take on the 'caretaker of the heart' job."

He tugged her close. "And?"

Standing between his legs, she placed her hands on his shoulders and stared down at him. "And she decided that no other Mulvane woman would fall beneath the chicanery of another male. She'd protect them from such tragedy."

"By thumping?"

Jillian watched his lips curve into another grin. "Granddad Mulvane used to say that his Morgana had the stubbornness of Aphrodite, and while Gwendolyn, my mother, had inherited my grandmother's beauty, she'd also inherited my grandmother's cunning."

"In what way?"

"Aunt Morgana always went along on whatever dates my mother had."

David waited for the punch line.

"But then my mother snuck out on other dates. Each time that she was married, my aunt never even knew the man existed until after the wedding. Grams said that after two such failures to do her job properly, Aunt Morgana resigned. With Mama. But by then, I had been born.''

David nodded slowly, comprehendingly. ''Morgana's haunting to protect you?''

''Right. And she doesn't like storms. She died during one when her car went around a curve too fast. So on stormy nights, she doesn't like to be alone. Sometimes she wanders downstairs and into the shop.''

He nuzzled her neck. ''To do what?'' he asked curiously before he realized that he was responding to her story as if he believed it.

''If a man and a woman are in the shop, the woman mysteriously is pinched on the backside.''

David chuckled. She had a great imagination. ''Does the poor sap get whacked?''

''Sometimes.'' She laughed softly against his ear. ''Cornelia Quinton was in the shop when Albert Putnam was here. Cornelia swung around to lambaste the person who'd pinched her, took one look at Albert, and fell in love.''

Head bent, he undid the top of her blouse. ''You spin a good tale.''

''Skeptic. But did you know that lightning won't strike during a thunderstorm if you get into a feather bed?''

Lightly he kissed the flesh he'd exposed. ''Why is it that the more I listen to your superstitions and stories, the more I begin to believe them?''

Jillian caressed his jaw. Beneath her fingers, she felt the short stubble of his beard. ''All of them or just that one?''

''That one made a lot of sense to me.''

"I must have missed something when I read your palm." As his tongue moistened her skin, excitement mingled with anticipation and skittered across her flesh in a warm shiver.

"Chilled?" he murmured against the corner of her mouth.

"Warm," she whispered. "I didn't notice that your Mount of Venus was overdeveloped."

"I have a feeling that's bad."

"Overfleshed and firm shows a person controlled by their sex drive."

"Bad, huh?"

She heard his smile. "No restraint."

David laughed. "On occasion."

"I'm glad you came tonight." She slid her hand down his arm and linked her fingers with his to tug him to a stand.

David followed her into the dark hall. "I came to protect you." He peered through the inky darkness, trying to see ahead of him. "Can you see where you're going?"

"We won't get lost."

"We need another candle," he insisted.

Jillian looked back over her shoulder at him. "I left some in the kitchen on the counter near the windows. Want me to get them?"

"I'll get them."

He wasn't gone a minute. Jillian watched him cautiously make his way back toward her.

"I couldn't find them."

"There was a box."

"Well, they're not there now. And it was pitch-dark in there. I thought we left a candle lit when we left?"

"Uh huh. We did."

"It's out. And I know I brought in my flashlight, but I can't find it now."

"Aunt Morgana."

"Jill, knock it off."

She smiled lazily when he stood close again. "She's probably upset that you're here."

Lightning flashed through a window, casting the room in a ghostly whiteness. As thunder rumbled overhead, he vowed not to let the eeriness of the weather get to him. "Too bad."

"Yes, too bad," she agreed lightly, coiling an arm around his neck. "She'll just have to accept . . ."

Her words trailed off as the thumping began again.

David drew back on a groan. "I don't believe this."

"Ignore her."

He shook his head. "No, I'm going to stop the racket. Now! I'll go close that damn shutter."

"David, it isn't a shutter."

"Whatever," he grumbled. "Where's the attic?"

"Why don't you just forget about it?"

The thumping grew louder.

"Your apparition is tenacious."

He released her so suddenly that she swayed.

"I'll be back as soon as I close the window. Where's the ladder to the attic?"

Jillian sighed. He was a stubborn man. "In the pantry off the kitchen. Take this candle, not that it will do you any good."

His fingers brushed hers in a sensuous caress. "I'll meet you in the bedroom. Five minutes," he called back.

* * *

The musty smell in the attic nauseated him. As he stood in the pitched-ceiling room, a chill swept over him. He held the candle out at arm's length and searched for a window.

There weren't any.

Just coldness.

And eerie silence.

The floorboards creaked beneath his feet. Overhead, thunder cracked as if determined to shake the house. Raising the candle above his head, he scanned the rafters for some sign of a hole or a loose board. He saw none.

It made no sense. The room was icy. Too cold for a summer night, even a stormy one with the wind howling outside and the rain pounding overhead.

Slowly turning, he peered at the dark walls. There had to be a hole somewhere in the narrow room. Or a branch had to be banging against the roof. There had to be some logical explanation for the cold and the noise.

He lifted the candle in front of him to get a better view. Like a shroud, cobwebs draped everything. He peered at the silhouettes of a full-length mirror, a trunk, an antique sewing machine, high-back chairs, and a seamstress's mannequin—

He stood in total darkness. It was as if someone had blown out the flame.

David drew a hard breath. He didn't believe in fortune-telling, tarot cards, casting the runes, or any of that other nonsense. Hell, he wasn't even sure that he believed in paranormal ability. And he sure didn't believe in ghosts, he told himself almost reassuringly as he inched his way in the black room toward the ladder.

He stepped down while looking for a logical explanation. The wind was coming in from somewhere. It had snuffed the flame. It—

As he stepped onto the next ladder rung, like the breath of a wintery gust, bone-chilling coldness suddenly swept down over him again. He looked up into the darkness as if compelled to, then started to reach for the hatch to close it. But his fingers never touched it.

With a bang, the hatch slammed down.

Chapter Nine

Jillian fluffed a pillow behind her and listened to the raging storm. Rain drummed against the roof, the wind keened a song, and lightning lit the bedroom for a second, but she felt none of the disturbance. She'd never been afraid during storms. She liked the excitement of sound that came from the pelting rain and the cracking of thunder. She liked the way the sky lit up as if some special celebration were taking place in the universe. It was, she mused. Here and now within her house. Hearing David's approaching footsteps, a peaceful excitement settled over her. She focused on the bedroom doorway and waited for him to appear. "What did you find?"

"Cold. There must be a hole in the roof somewhere."

"Your candle is—"

"Out," he quipped, sitting on the bed and tugging off his pants.

Jillian cuddled deeper beneath the blanket. Morgana was obviously still at it.

The chill wouldn't go away. David slid under the covers beside her and inched close for body heat.

"You *are* cold." When he didn't respond with even a grunt, she shifted to see his face. "Did Morgana bother you?"

"This house is not haunted," he declared. "I don't believe in ghosts."

She sighed at his stubbornness. "What do you believe in?"

In the darkened room, her skin appeared alabaster, translucent like some cold statue. But beneath his fingers, her thigh was smooth and warm. "What I can touch." He brought his face closer. "See." His lips coursed the curve of her shoulder then trailed along her jaw. "Taste," he said against her mouth. "This is real."

"If you keep doing that and . . ."

"And this?" He kissed her collarbone then ran his tongue in a caress across her breast.

She closed her eyes. "I'll want more."

"Seems fair—since I want you. Maybe, I have for a long time," he whispered.

She arched against him as he drew the nipple into his mouth. Slowly, leisurely, his tongue circled it. On a sigh, Jillian pressed him closer to her. With a tracing of his tongue, he stirred her to the edge of insanity and brewed a storm within her to rival the one raging outside. When his gentleness left and the demand of passion began, she couldn't say. But as he

spread nibbling kisses downward and then retraced the
path, her skin quivered. Pleasure and torment mingled together. Want blended with need. With a slow-
ness that threatened to drive her mad, he entered her.
With an urgency that she matched, he took her away
from reality. He hurled her past stars, beyond everything she knew as tangible. Arms and legs tangled together. Her universe centered on one man, and the
explosion he brought into her life. This was real. For
both of them. Here, they moved together. And nothing else mattered. Here, they soared to a world more
mystical than any other. A place where thoughts gave
way to sensations, where the differences between them
no longer existed. And willingly she followed him.
Desperately she clung to hold him there. Lovingly she
ached to never leave the magical kingdom only he
seemed capable of creating for her.

She was warm and comforting. The chill within him
had long passed. He dodged pondering what he'd felt
in the attic. Sunshine and warmth were with him in the
dark room. The woman beside him lit up his world.

Jillian cuddled closer. "I feel wonderful."

He kissed her collarbone.

"Do you think life can be too good sometimes?"

On a laugh, he nuzzled her neck. "There's nothing
wrong with that."

"I hope not," she said on a sigh.

"You could evoke a hex on us."

"I'd fail."

Eyes still closed, he kissed her shoulder. Her scent
was there, too, its fragrance a familiar one now.
"Why?"

"Because my cosmo energies are crossing each other."

David chuckled. "Sometimes, darling, you talk batty."

She snuggled closer as he draped a leg over her hip and tugged her to him. "See. There's the problem."

"No problem."

"How can you say that?"

Lazily, he kissed her jaw. "Because I'll accept batty in you, if you'll accept that sometimes I act like a pompous ass."

"Not you," she teased.

"Go with this. Don't analyze."

"Do you hear yourself?" she asked on a laugh.

"Yes."

"David, we're different."

"Thankfully."

Instinctively she smiled again. "I meant our needs are different."

"I don't think so."

"You won't be serious, will you?"

"It's not the right time for serious."

Jillian kissed the base of his throat. "But our needs *are* different."

"Our wants aren't."

"No, they aren't," she whispered. The soft hair on his chest brushed her cheek.

As the moist tip of her tongue glided across his flesh, David pressed his head into the pillow and closed his eyes. "Don't look at the future this time," he murmured.

Her hand skimmed his belly. "Don't you want to know?"

"No," he managed huskily. "Forget the future and the past. All that matters is—"

"Now," she murmured and needed no more response from him than his soft moan.

"I found my flashlight," he said while draining bacon on a paper towel the next morning.

"Where?"

David squinted against the morning sunlight to watch her cut up a banana. "Outside the bedroom door."

Jillian held back a giggle.

"No comment?"

"None needed," she returned, grinning.

"Here." David held out a strip of bacon. "One tiny piece."

"Too much cholesterol. I give in to junk food only during moments of extreme weakness."

He grimaced as she added sliced bananas to a yogurt concoction in the blender. "What harm can it cause you?"

"None, now. But in years to come—"

As she shook her head firmly, he turned away with a shrug to answer the telephone. "You think too much about the future."

"One of my best traits," she mumbled more to herself than to him before concentrating to hear his side of the conversation.

"Your real-estate agent," he yelled over the noisy whirling of the blender.

As they passed each other, she dodged his hand's quick lunge at her hair.

David flicked off the blender switch and poured her morning feast into a glass. The fruit and yogurt he could stand. But he'd seen her toss in dashes of six different herbs and spices. He sniffed, trying to distinguish the strong smell. Garlic seemed predominant.

Setting down the receiver, she smiled at him. "I have good news."

"What's in this?" he asked, gesturing with his thumb toward the glass.

"You watched me prepare it."

"No—no. What else did you put in it? A dash of what and what?"

"Cinnamon, rose petals—"

He grimaced.

"Mint leaves, garlic—"

He held up a halting hand. "Never mind. You drink it. I'll stick to bacon and eggs."

Jillian grinned as he settled at the table and looked almost lovingly at his plate. "I have good news. Carol's found a building for me."

"If no one whips it out from under you."

"Oh, David, don't be a pessimist. I'm going over there right after breakfast."

"Where is it?"

"Not far," she said, whirling away.

"Where?"

"Off the lake. That's good," she added brightly. "I'll be in the natural pathway of tourists."

When she kept her back to him, he insisted, "Where off the lake?"

"Near Grover's Pier."

He jabbed his eggs with a fork and watched the yolk spill onto his plate. The only building he knew near Grover's Pier was a shack. He shook his head. She was too sharp to invest good money in something that would crumble beneath a good wind. "Will you be free by this evening?"

With her tongue, she wiped away the mustache left by her drink. "What did you have in mind?"

He chuckled. She looked twelve years old. "Dinner. I had dinner in mind."

"I'm always agreeable to dinner."

"At Agnes's home," he said more seriously.

Jillian sipped at her drink. "You're insane."

David leaned back in the chair and shifted to stretch his legs out. "I accepted the invitation weeks ago. She said that I could bring a guest."

Jillian frowned. "She doesn't mean me."

"There's no one else I want to be with." He set down his fork. "Will you go?"

She wouldn't let ghosts from the past haunt them, she told herself. If he dared to exorcise his, then she could do the same. "I'm no coward. I'll go," she said with a feigned laugh and hoped he hadn't noticed her trembling hand when she'd set down her glass. "But you're not as stable as I thought."

He closed the distance between them. "More than you," he teased to keep her mood light, to keep himself from thinking about the consequences of his taking Jillian with him. He curled his lip at the drink before her. "*That* even smells disgusting."

She avoided nothing, David realized while driving home. She charged toward opposition as if relishing it. He'd been dodging it for days. Walking into the house, he could hear his brother singing a duet with a pop singer.

Lately, like two ships passing in the night, when David had been home, Matt hadn't been. Though David would have rather had a serious talk with his free-spirited brother sooner, he'd felt that they needed time to cool tense emotions. Following the sound of the blaring music, he entered the kitchen and switched off the radio.

Matt swung around, looking ready for battle. "Oh." He grinned. "You actually *do* live here."

David responded with a wry grin.

"I figured you've been avoiding me," Matt added.

David shook his head. "I've been busy. Sorry." He poured a cup of coffee then sipped the thick dark brew. When had his brother made it? Yesterday morning? And he'd probably kept it warm all day. Matt still waltzed through life without too much concern for the next day. Problems didn't exist because he had a tendency to play the ostrich. His motto was clear. If he didn't pay attention to the problems, they'd go away. Life should be so simple, David mused. Grimacing at the coating on his tongue, he quickly swallowed another mouthful of the coffee then dumped the rest in the sink. "Could we put this off—our talk—a little longer?"

"Sure." Matt shrugged. "Now or later, it doesn't matter. I'm not going to change my mind, though. And you aren't either, are you?"

David held his hands out to him in an appealing gesture. "Let's not talk about it today. Have you got a little free time? I have about an hour," he said with a glance at his watch. When Matt continued to stare quizzically at him, he persisted, "How about a game of handball?"

Matt pulled back. "I'm not betting on my future."

"No, bets. Just a nice brotherly game." David grinned slowly. "A friendly game of handball."

Matt snorted. "You're too damn competitive for it to be friendly. But I can give you a run for your money," he said cockily.

David tossed a kitchen towel at him. "You're on, hotshot. Dry the dishes from your breakfast while I change."

Matt sauntered past him. "One question."

"Yeah?"

"Where did you eat breakfast?"

David turned away.

"Are you sure that you're up to a game of anything today?" he jibed. "You might be too tired."

A man who's floating can't get tired, David mused then laughed out loud.

"What did you say?" Matt asked.

David headed toward the swinging door. "You're going to lose as usual."

"Why?" Matt yelled.

"I feel like a winner today," David called back. Prepared for anything.

He wasn't prepared for Jillian. During the previous night with the shadows slanting across her flesh, her hair tousled, her complexion flushed from passion, he thought that she'd never look quite so beautiful again. He'd been wrong. As he stood in her doorway that evening, his breath caught in his throat. Her hair was pulled back and held in place with two silver combs. Skin he knew and had touched and had tasted looked even paler against the thin-strapped, black silk top. Her waist appeared small enough for one arm to circle. Stepping into the hallway, he tested the idea. The silk of her white skirt rustled beneath the brush of his pant legs. David stared into her face. How could he have walked past her beauty all those years? Or was the beauty he was finally seeing more than the vision before him? He knew the woman beneath the loveliness. He'd seen her generosity, her vivacity, he'd felt her compassion. He doubted another woman would ever compare.

"Hi," she said softly.

"Hi, yourself. You look—you look—"

"Proper?"

"Beautiful."

Jillian clung to him. "You'll make me blush."

"You make me ache."

A teasing spirit swept over her. She lifted a brow. "Do you need a drink to calm you?"

"That wasn't what I had in mind."

She slipped from his embrace. "I took out the Scotch."

David walked over to the counter and opened the ice bucket. "Do you want one?"

"No, I need a clear mind tonight."

Ice cubes clinked against the glass. "Did you get the building?"

"Yes." Her face brightened. "It's perfect."

He smiled at the excitement he heard in her voice. Lately she'd faced a great many obstacles and had met each of them with a bright disposition, a sunny smile and a determination that stirred admiration. He understood adversity. Some people succumbed to it. He'd thought them foolish. And while he'd handled his with hard work, he'd nurtured a tinge of bitterness through the years. She hadn't. But she did possess a fair amount of mistrust, a caution that seemed otherwise out of character. He smiled to himself, realizing that weeks ago he'd thought her impulsive and zany.

"So one problem is out of the way," she said.

David snapped back to his surroundings. If he'd blinked, he wouldn't have seen her quick-passing frown of concern. "More than one. Soon," he assured her. "I checked back with Clyde Vale. I'm going to see him tomorrow." He ran a comforting hand down her arm. "Don't worry, Andy will be all right."

She offered a weak smile but pressed her body against him as if seeking some kind of support. "Why is it that your reassurance makes me feel better even though every reading I did for Andy indicated the same thing?"

He tightened his arm at her waist. "Tell me."

Her head thrown back, she smiled impishly. "Because I know that you're keeping the red scarf with you now?" she teased.

He laughed. "How easy you make everything seem."

She ran her hands over the strong planes of his face as his lips nipped hers. She loved him but... She stopped the rest of her thought as one kiss blended into another. Even as he drew back, she felt the heat of his kiss lingering and knew every memory she had with him would do the same when the end came.

"Agnes isn't going to let up," he said seriously before turning back to pour his glass of Scotch.

"The poor woman."

"Poor?"

"In the important things." She glanced at the clock.
"Agnes is never happy, David. I don't ever remember
her happy, even when her husband was alive. It makes
you wonder what soured her years ago."

He took a good swallow. "Don't be so damn understanding of her. She isn't of you."

"I can afford to be."

"Why?"

She moved up close behind him and put her arms
around his waist. "I'm happy."

"Any special reason?" he asked, facing her.

As he tugged her closer, Jillian laughed. "You."

They arrived late. Not the best way to start an evening at Agnes's home, Jillian reflected the moment she
saw Agnes. She glared at Jillian and then steam-
rollered toward them. Jillian suddenly felt invincible.

Facing David, Agnes angled her body so Jillian
stared at her back. Jillian had been snubbed before by
Agnes but never quite so deliberately. "I'm glad that
you came, David," the older woman said. "I've been
worrying about you. You haven't been acting like
yourself for weeks."

With an arm around Jillian's shoulder, David
shifted, forcing Agnes to face both of them. "Or just
the opposite."

The woman's mouth noticeably tightened. She
drilled David with a look that would have bored a hole
through a lesser man then offered them her back and

strolled away to greet new guests. Jillian considered the courage he'd shown. All his life he'd worked to be accepted by this woman and others like her. And now he jeopardized everything because she stood beside him. Discreetly she nudged him with her elbow. "You didn't expect the welcome mat for me, did you?"

"A friendly face."

"Foolish man," she jibed and linked her arm with his. "Come on. I do see a friendly face."

"Where?" As she directed him to look across the room at Myra, he touched the small of her back to urge her forward. Beneath his hand, he felt her tenseness. If she was nervous, she hid it admirably. During the next half hour, she charmed the socks off the governor. Looking captivated, he kept nodding his head agreeably while she discussed the Ptolemaic concept of the universe.

"Some people seem to still believe that the earth is the center of the universe," Jillian finished.

"Did you say you own a local shop?" he questioned.

"The Stargazer. A place for dreamy thoughts about the future," she answered absently, looking past David.

Frowning, David looked over his shoulder to see what had distracted her. Agnes's butler stood beside him.

"Mrs. Simpson would like to see you in the study, sir."

Jillian gave David's arm a squeeze. "Good luck."

Standing by shelves of books, Agnes held a leather-bound volume and faced him with one of her stern, unyielding stares. "I wanted time alone to talk to you." She lifted her chin and gave him a tight-lipped, pleased smile.

He felt like a man who was facing a firing squad. In the past, he had ignored her clipped tone. Now it annoyed him. When he was young, a bank officer had used the same supercilious manner with his mother when she'd gone to him for a loan.

"I believe you'll be pleased to learn that the town council met. I've just finished talking to the mayor. You were their unanimous choice to fill the council's vacancy. Young blood is needed, David. And you have always displayed impeccable behavior. I know that the town's best interest is as important to you as it is to the rest of us."

Instead of pleasure, tension rippled through him. Why did he feel as if another shoe was being dangled in her fingers and ready to drop?

She placed the book back in its slot on the shelf and then strolled toward the door. "Several of the members of the town council have organized a list of businesses that we'd prefer didn't renew leases." She waved a hand as if pushing away something insignificant like a fly. "You, of course, will know the legal ramifications. However, I see no problem. They can find buildings for their stores in one of the other towns, some fisherman's haven. But Lakeside is becoming quite exclusive. We'd like to nurture a community for the higher class."

David took his cue and followed her. More than anything, curiosity was leading him. What was she up to this time? he wondered. Years ago while in law school, he'd learned that timely silences sometimes gave him the edge.

"You haven't forgotten my special request, have you?"

Without difficulty, David deduced that they were discussing Jillian's house. "No, I haven't."

Her lips curved upward in a semblance of a smile. "I thought not. At first, I was surprised to see you with her. But then, it occurred to me that you'd thought of another way to convince her to sell the house. Surely," she said in a voice that almost purred, "you can persuade her." She surveyed the guests then focused on Jillian. "You obviously are still considering ways to do that."

"Why would you think that?"

Her head down, she adjusted the narrow silk cuff on her dress. "What other reason would you have for seeing her? Certainly you have nothing in common." She cast a look toward her guests and visually zeroed in on a town council member. "You must excuse me now."

"She won't sell," David said firmly.

"You'll find a way to convince her." She placed a hand on his arm and shot another tight-lipped smile at him. "I know I can count on you, David. We're two of a kind."

Stunned, he stared after her. He wasn't like her. Across the room, his eyes met Jillian's. At her frowning face, a mimicking one, he forced himself to offer a wry smile. He considered all the years that he'd have done anything to get what he'd wanted. That was before, he told himself. Not anymore. He had what he wanted most of all. Passing a white-jacketed servant with a tray, he grabbed a champagne glass then wound his way around couples to reach Jillian on the other side of the room. Halfway across the room, he was cornered by one of the council members.

Seeing him trapped, Jillian wandered toward the foyer. He looked so troubled when he'd come out of the room with Agnes. Was he now regretting that he'd brought her? Jillian wondered. He wanted this lifestyle, she reminded herself as she glanced up at the teardrop chandelier. The wealth was secondary to him. She understood enough of the pain he'd suffered in his youth to recognize how important respectability and social standing in the community were to him.

Meandering through the foyer, she stared at the individual portraits of every Simpson. At eye level on the wall near the foot of the stairs was a Simpson family portrait of William and his younger brother, Hugh, with their parents. Jillian stared at the painting of her father. William had been a handsome man with a smile in his eyes, but he'd sat as rigid in his chair as his father and brother. Hadn't her mother seen how wrong he was for her? She'd been so young when she'd met him. Had she expected him to accept her? Had she really believed that she could blend into his life?

Visually she circled the room with its priceless antiques, heavy brocade wallpaper and damask drapes. None of this would have mattered to her mother. Acceptance, yes, but not by everyone. All she'd ever longed for was a love that was strong enough to accept and understand her always. She stared at her father's portrait a moment longer then turned around to find David. Agnes blocked her view of the guests.

"I didn't think you'd have the nerve to come."

Jillian realized she felt nothing toward the woman before her—not even dislike. They hardly knew each other. If anything, because of that, she was—and had always been—a little puzzled by Agnes's manner toward her. "You convinced Lillian to file that complaint against the Stargazer, didn't you?"

"She's a good friend. She does as I ask."

"Everyone does, don't they?"

"It's high time that you learned that. David told me that you're refusing to sell the house."

Jillian released an impatient sigh. "Why do you want it?"

Across the room, David nodded agreeably as Lakeside's loquacious mayor expounded about highway repairs. Spotting Jillian, he started to inch himself away from the mayor. While the man continued as if he were on a podium, David reminded himself that he'd made a promise to her that she wouldn't stand alone. It was a promise he planned on keeping. Excusing himself, he quickly weaved his way through people.

"You're just like your mother," Agnes flared finally before whirling around and nearly knocking a vase from a table.

Still digesting what Agnes had said, Jillian stared dumbly after her. What had her mother done to Agnes? she wondered. Seconds passed before she realized that David was beside her.

"Jill?"

Responding to the firm pressure of his fingers, she sent him a smile that was meant to ease the tension from his face. "Hi."

"Hi, yourself. Did you have a showdown?"

"Sort of." She gave him a wry smile. "I'm sorry, but I can't stay for dinner."

He grinned down at her and planted a kiss on her brow. "Is that all you do? Think about your stomach?"

The ridiculousness of his response made her genuinely laugh.

"How about a juicy hamburger at Louie's Diner?" he suggested.

"And then?" she asked expectantly.

He urged her toward the door. "Then we'll go to my place."

Smiling, she slid her arm around his waist. "Why not mine?"

"Aunt Morgana needs to rest," he teased.

Chapter Ten

Jillian pushed another French fry through the puddle of mustard on her plate. "Agnes is going to make trouble for you, David."

He sipped coffee cautiously. He was more concerned with her previous quietness than what he'd have to face later. "What did she say to you?"

She let out an uneven breath. "She told me that I was just like my mother."

"Not a revelation to you, is it?"

"No. But I never viewed myself as a disruptive force."

"I would," he said, grinning.

He made her smile despite a serious mood. "Have I disrupted your life?"

"Pleasantly." He reached across the table for her hand. "What else did she say?"

Jillian raised his hand to her mouth and kissed his knuckles. "She has such anger toward anyone with the Mulvane name. She seemed almost illogical at times."

"Why?"

"She said Mama lived in a dream world. That's true, in a way. She realized how different she was and knew she couldn't lead a life quite like everyone else. Instead of fighting it, she nurtured it. I suppose my grandparents nudged her along."

David remained quiet. He'd seen too much anger in Agnes's face, too much disbelief in Jillian's earlier to believe more hadn't been said.

Jillian felt her throat tighten. "I don't know how anyone who'd known my mother could believe that she didn't care about someone else's feelings."

"Is that what Agnes said?"

Jillian nodded. "She claimed that Mama never cared about anyone." Jillian met his eyes. "That's not true. Sometimes I think her biggest weakness was that she cared too much about other people. But Agnes insisted that if Mama had shown any concern for William, then she'd never have married him. She was so bitter when she spoke to me, David. She said that my mother ruined his chances for a political future."

"The Simpsons probably had lofty aspirations for him. But he might never have run for office. She has no way of knowing that."

"No, she doesn't. But she believes that. She told me that she wouldn't rest until she ruined every Mulvane in town. She'll prove to everyone that William made a mistake years ago when he married Mama."

David squeezed her hand. He didn't want her hurt anymore. He wouldn't let anyone hurt her, he decided. For as long as she'd let him, he'd be near. He loved her. Simple words, but if spoken seriously, he sensed that he might send her running. "How do you and Andy figure in this?"

"If Andy and I became successful then we'd make her look bad." She smiled wryly. "David, she's been trying to discredit the Mulvane name for years. If she can't do that, then people will question her opinion. She has to prove that she's right about us."

He looked down at his plate and the congealed gravy on the roast beef. "She's more vindictive than I thought."

"I also know why she wants the house. I don't think she intended to tell me, but she became so angry that she lost control. The town council was approached by the National History Society. My house and the others on Raven Lane are going to be declared historical landmarks."

"And she wants the prestige of owning all of them." He shook his head. "The woman craves power." He waited until Jillian's eyes met his. "But she's forgetting one thing. You're not alone."

Her breath came out unevenly. If desire were the only emotion, how simple time with him would be. But another emotion—love—complicated every moment that they spent together. "Tomorrow, you might think differently," she reminded him.

"I won't," he assured her softly.

A tightness in her throat promised tears. How much she wanted to cling to his words, she realized.

David gestured toward the window. "Look at the sky." As she raised her face, he ran the back of a knuckle over her cheek. "No clouds."

Jillian grabbed his optimistic mood to heart. "What a beautiful moon."

His head tilted back with laughter. "Any other superstitions about the moon?" he asked, grateful for her ability to draw on humor during a dark moment.

"Plant peas when the moon is full." She hunched forward and framed his face with her hands. She kissed him soundly for his easy acceptance, his enjoyment of the silly beliefs that people had always sent her grandmother strange looks for spouting. "Point at the moon," she added. "It's good luck."

"I just got all the good luck I need."

She clucked her tongue. "I definitely should read your palm again. I did miss something."

"What?"

"A tendency toward overindulgence."

"I don't need to read your palm to know that you have a very hypnotic way about you during storms."

"Only during storms?" she asked.

The look she gave him nearly curled his toes. "On several other occasions, too."

"Like when the moon is full," she said with a glance out the window.

"I believe so." He gestured with his fork at her plate. "Finished?"

"Tired?" she asked.

"No."

"Needing your rest?"

"No."

She giggled. "Just want to go to bed?"

"You *are* psychic." He reached for his wallet. "We're going to have to endure Morgana again," he said while scanning the bill. "I forgot my brother is staying at my place."

"I knew that."

"Quit mind reading."

Her eyes sparkled. "You're an open book."

"Did you know that I have to get an early start tomorrow morning?"

"Then you should go to bed early."

"My thought exactly," he said, sliding out of the booth and then tugging her to a stand.

"I'll shove you out the door at daybreak."

It was past ten before he left her house. While she headed for her new store, David made Andy his top priority.

He stopped at the local diner for a cup of coffee then crossed the street to his office. Yawning, he strolled in an hour later than usual.

Without a word, Myra held messages out to him.

"So many?"

"You've been out of the office a lot lately."

"I guess," he mumbled, standing beside Myra's desk.

"Seems kind of unnatural for a workaholic."

David looked up from sorting through the messages. "Did you type up the Kingford will?"

"It's all ready for signing."

"Call Mr. Kingford for me and set up an appointment."

"For when?"

"Anytime but today. I have to leave the office."

"All day?"

"I hope to wrap up the Mulvane case without having to go to trial."

Myra hunched forward. "Can you clear him?"

David dropped the messages back on her desk. "I'm going to try."

"Matt called about ten minutes ago and wanted to talk to you. Didn't you two reach an understanding yet?"

"We're not growling at each other," he answered.

"That's a good sign. I was beginning to wonder how you two could pass each other every morning and not talk. But I guess the Mulvane case is keeping you busy." Curiosity edged her voice. "Before a trial you have to confer with your client often. Jillian, too," she added, not too cleverly.

He gave her an easy smile. "I bet you wanted to be a spy when you were a little girl?"

"I still do," she quipped.

"Mata Hari would have come in second." He tapped the telephone on her desk with his finger. "Get Agnes on the phone for me."

"What a way to start the day."

Jillian spent the morning dismantling display counters. Shelves of herbs and potion bottles were wrapped in tissue and packed in a crate. Her back aching from bending over the box, she straightened and stretched. The job was a boring one that she'd wished she'd never had to experience. But life tossed people curves. A month ago, she hadn't expected to be packing and moving to a new shop. A month ago, she hadn't expected David to be in her life. What she felt for him wasn't simple. Love, she admitted honestly.

But she couldn't forget that every time her mother had loved she'd lost.

Across the room, Iris Ogilvy unshelved books and set them on a table for her. Jillian smiled. She'd gained many friends, people like Iris who'd shown up minutes ago, volunteering to help her pack.

"I planned to buy this book," she said, holding up *The Crystal Readings*. "But I knew I wouldn't have time to read it." She pulled a face. "I've been urging fate's good luck towards my daughter and her husband. That's a full-time job."

"How was their dinner out?"

She beamed back at Jillian. "I do believe I'll be able to read the book now."

"Good."

"They miraculously came to the conclusion that they haven't been talking to each other. Isn't that amazing," she added. "Everything is better now." She scurried toward Jillian. "I emptied all the books on the top three shelves, but I have to go now to start dinner."

Jillian nodded. "Thank you. And take that book."

"Oh, I couldn't do that."

"Please."

"You're a sweet thing," Iris said, passing by and patting Jillian's cheek. "I might just have to nudge you, too."

Worriedly Jillian looked after her. "Nudge?"

Iris sent Jillian a sly smile. "Toward a handsome lawyer." At a sudden thump overhead, she paused and looked up. "What's that noise?"

Your opposition. "A shutter," Jillian said.

* * *

David hurried out of Clyde Vale's store. The pieces of the puzzle were finally fitting together.

He made one stop during his drive back to Lakeside. Even before he braked his Jeep, Andy was hurrying out of his auto-parts store to meet him.

Five minutes later as David was leaving Andy, he considered the consequences of what he planned to do. He was going to make waves. He was going to disrupt certain lives. He might hurt his law practice. It was a chance that he had to take, he told himself while he parked in front of the sheriff's office.

Jillian pushed down the flaps on another carton. At the tinkling of the shop bell, she looked up. Surprise mingled with wariness. Straightening her back, she attempted to calm her nerves as she faced Agnes.

"I heard you found another building." Agnes scanned the room with a look of disdain. "Where is it?"

"Grover's Pier."

An amused smile twisted her lips. "You bought the old barn? You really bought *that*? You are a foolish dreamer. What sane person would risk entering that shack?"

Jillian leaned back against the banister. How many times had she pondered the woman's animosity? Too often, Jillian mused. She'd wasted entirely too much time wondering why Agnes disliked her. "I'll make it work," she responded firmly.

Agnes swung a look back at her. "So determined. William was always so sure of himself, so positive that what he was doing was right. He would have gone far," she said almost wistfully.

Jillian tipped her head questioningly.

"I would have helped him. *I* would have been perfect for him."

Jillian took a step closer, trying to understand what she was really saying.

As if she were alone, Agnes stared with distant eyes out one of the long, narrow windows. "I couldn't believe he'd turn his back on me like that."

"Turn his back on you?"

Her head swiveled toward Jillian. For a second, she just stared then her eyes refocused on Jillian. "Yes," she flared. "He was supposed to marry me."

"Marry?"

"Do you find that so hard to believe?" She released a quick brittle laugh. "I was the right one for him. I was the one his family expected him to marry. But then he met her. She turned his head. Like you've done to David. You're ruining his life just as your mother ruined William's."

Jillian shook her head. "That's not true. My mother—"

"Was a witch."

As a satisfied look settled on Agnes's face, Jillian knew she'd paled. But a second had passed before she'd realized that Agnes was serious. "You can't believe that."

"Denying it doesn't change anything." With a glance at the carnelian and the rose quartz on the display counter, she issued what sounded like a challenge to Jillian. "You'll never open that store."

Anger rocked Jillian, but she kept her voice steady. "I'll open it."

"And I'll help her," Andy suddenly said from the doorway.

Agnes whipped around and strolled toward him on the way out the door. "You'll be in jail," she flared.

"Agnes?" Jillian waited for the woman's eyes to meet hers. "The bottom line is that you're not running the Mulvanes out of town. Ever," Jillian added softly.

Andy released a long whistle the moment that the door closed behind Agnes.

For all her bravado, Jillian felt a tremble move through her. "I always feel as if I've passed through a tornado after talking to her," she said unevenly.

"Yeah." Andy grinned at her.

"I can't believe that someone as intelligent as she is could be so ignorant to parapsychology."

Andy touched her shoulder. "Hey, lots of people are scared of what they don't understand."

"Yes, but—" She noted the sparkle in his eyes. "Something's happened?"

He beamed. "I'm cleared."

Jillian gripped his upper arms. "Are you sure?"

"I'm sure."

"Oh, Andy." She threw her arms around his neck and hugged him. "Thank God." At his laugh, she drew back to see his face. "What happened?"

"David stopped at the shop and told me that he had the evidence to clear me."

"David—" She looked past him and frowned. "Why isn't he with you?"

"He said that he had some unfinished business at the sheriff's office."

Jillian frowned. "Why would he go there if you're—"

"He said that the charges were dropped against me," he assured her, then grinned boyishly. "You told me everything· would be okay. I kept remembering that."

Jillian nodded. "Mama would have said that it was in the cards. The King came up."

He gave her an uncomprehending look.

"It signifies a man of quiet energy and steadfastness. Successful in business," she added. "You know how Mama would have interpreted that. She would have said that you and I alone couldn't straighten out this mess."

"That's why you insisted on going to see David?"

Jillian nodded.

"I'm glad you did."

"Me, too," she answered. During a difficult time in her life, David had brought her more happiness than she'd ever expected. "Me, too," she repeated.

Moonlight slanted across the roof of her house by the time David arrived. He found Jillian perched on a ladder in the Stargazer and stretching to unhook one of the giant spheres from its lofty position. "Damn." Quickly David skirted one of the crates surrounding her. "What are you doing? Couldn't you wait for help?"

Jillian gasped at the firm, unexpected grip of his arm around her hip. "You could have scared me to death sneaking up on me like that," she shot back but relaxed against him.

His hands remained firm on her waist as he lifted her down. "You have a habit of taking risks and trying to break your neck. I'll take that down for—"

"Forget that," she chided, her mouth hovering close to his. "For Andy, thank you," she murmured against his lips.

Why did success this time seem so much better? he wondered. Why was a kiss from her better than all the praise he'd ever received? He had it bad, he realized. Somehow, at sometime, he'd fallen head over heels in love with the woman. "How did you know about Andy?"

A languid, relaxed sensation as if she were drugged floated over her. Breathless, she opened her eyes to slits. "He came to see me."

"He should have stayed and helped you take down those decorations."

Snuggling, she ran a hand up his chest. "You have a tendency to be a worrywart."

"Without me, you'd have fallen—"

She pulled a face. "Back to the ladder, again?"

"You take too many chances. You could have fallen off that ladder."

"With your help, I almost did."

At her annoyed look, he squeezed her for a second. "But it got you where I wanted you."

"Not breathing?"

David laughed, releasing his tight embrace. "In my arms."

"Sneaky, aren't you?"

"Me and Macavity." He glanced around. "Where is that cat? He's usually underfoot."

"He's been busy—for days," she said, slipping out of his embrace and then leading the way into the kitchen. "Macavity is on the prowl." At the sight of two bottles of champagne on the kitchen table, she smiled over her shoulder at him. "Two houses away. He's rendezvousing with a calico. You've been busy, too. Andy said that you went to see the sheriff." A hint of a frown pinched her brows. "All the charges have been dropped against Andy, haven't they?"

"Uh huh. I contacted a private investigator in Milwaukee to talk to the owner of the Farleyville building. The owner had no idea where Earl Siverson was."

Jillian reached into a cupboard for two tulip-shaped glasses. "He used that name to rent the property?"

David nodded. "The sheriff issued a warrant for Siverson's arrest under his real name Joe Bowden."

"Why did you go to the sheriff's office later?"

"I needed to talk to him about something that Clyde Vale had told me."

She faced him with an expectant look.

David took the glasses from her. "Vale gave an accurate description of Siverson. It matched Andy's. But one thing has been bothering me all along." David uncorked one bottle. "Who tipped off the sheriff's office to check on Andy's shop?"

Jillian leaned back against the kitchen counter.

"Somone had to be in cahoots with Siverson." He poured champagne into a glass. "After Vale realized that he had stolen merchandise, he called the sheriff's department."

Jillian joined him at the table. "And filed a statement?"

"That's right. But there wasn't any record of it," he told her.

Jillian inclined her head questioningly. "And?"

"Riley never filed it, because he was taking a kick-back from Siverson."

Jillian sank to a chair. For a moment, she felt too dumbfounded to say anything. The first thought to fully register in her mind slipped out. "Agnes."

"What?"

"Does Agnes know?"

"Save your concern," he said, annoyed, and handed a glass to her. "She wanted to close up Andy's shop. So Riley sent Siverson to Andy."

"It was a setup?"

"Riley was trying to frame him."

Jillian shook her head. "Agnes didn't know any of that, did she?"

"Not about Riley being involved in the stolen parts deal. But she urged him to get something on Andy."

"How do you know this?"

"Riley's hoping to turn state's evidence against Bowden, alias Siverson, and get a deal, so he's singing."

"I still feel sorry for her."

"You're a bigger person than I am."

"She's never gotten over being hurt, David. A woman who feels scorned rarely does."

David's head reared back.

"She expected William to marry her."

"What!"

"Yes," Jillian confirmed. "And she never forgave Mama for taking him from her."

"That doesn't make sense. She is a Simpson. She married Hugh."

"He wasn't the one that she wanted. She wanted my father. And she didn't marry Hugh until after my parents were married." Jillian weighed her next words. They sounded even implausible to her. "She was the one who ridiculed Mama the loudest, made fun of her. But she said something odd. She called Mama a witch."

"It's just an expression." Seeing her concern, he tried to make light of the term. "It means nothing."

"She believes it."

"Come on, Jill."

"She believes they exist. She thinks that he wouldn't have turned away from her unless Mama had cast a spell over him."

"Jill, that's crazy. Agnes is a sensible woman. She sits on the town council. Hell, last year she scoffed at the idea of a Christmas parade having a Santa Claus."

"She believes in witches."

He shook his head.

"It's true, David. That's why she wants me out of town."

"Salem revisited?"

She smiled weakly. "Something like that." Her voice saddened again. "Oh, David, I feel so sorry for her. She's always been so controlled by what other people thought of her. She's always worried about gossip and scandal, and now look what's happened. The newspaper will print the story about Riley, about her instigating this. What she'd feared most—scandal—will surround her."

He rounded the table and grabbed her hand. "And she'll deserve it." As she stood beside him, he kissed the tip of her nose. "That's her fate."

Her head fell back with her laugh. "Fate? Do you believe in fate?"

"Yes. I believe you and I were meant to be together."

At the intensity she saw in his eyes, she trembled and wasn't sure why.

He curled his hands around her shoulders. "I love you. I want to marry you."

Her smile faded at his serious tone. Stunned, Jillian stared at him. Why had she believed he'd never say those words to her? Why did her heart jump? Why did she want to say yes? Too many emotions suddenly rushed forward within her, the most dominant one was panic.

At her silence, he attempted a lightness that he didn't feel. "That wasn't meant to leave you speechless," he said quietly but tightened his hands on her upper arms until she looked up at him. "You can't say this is sudden," he coaxed.

It was. She loved him, but she never considered that emotion to include any real commitment. Her mother had never been lucky with that kind of commitment. Jillian had never imagined making it to anyone. So many times, she'd seen the heartbreak her mother had gone through because she believed in love, in sharing a lifetime with someone, in that ultimate sense of oneness. She'd never been as one with any of her husbands. Always, she'd stood apart. Jillian had never expected life to offer her anything else. She and her mother were alike—because they were different. "I hadn't thought about marriage," she said honestly.

"Neither had I before this but— Why are you ducking this?" he asked with a mirthless smile.

"I don't know if I'm ready for it. I don't think I'm cut out for marriage."

As she pulled away, David stared after her. She acted frightened. Oddly through storms and adversities, she'd never revealed such panic. He cursed himself for causing it, for not handling the moment right. For the first time in his life, he'd followed impulse then rushed forward without a hint of patience. Patience seemed impossible. His life, his future had been on the line with that one question. He'd said love, but she never had. What if she didn't love him? No, he didn't believe that. He'd held her, he'd felt the rush of not only passion but also love racing through her. Somehow he'd break down her resistance. Reason with her. Forget reasoning, he told himself. Reasoning had nothing to do with love. "Are you saying that you don't love me?"

"You have standards that—"

"To hell with the standards."

"You'll expect me to behave differently, think differently. I'm not sure that I can. Be logical," she appealed.

"Logical?" The word sounded ironic coming from her. "What's logic got to do with love? With us? All that matters is what we feel."

"No, it's not all that matters." A chill raced through her. She leaned back against the refrigerator, to keep from running she realized. "My mother taught me that love isn't that simple. David, she tried four times."

"You're not her."

She drew a hard breath. "But I am. I am like her. And I learned from Jason—"

"I'm not him."

"But you'll expect—"

"Nothing, dammit. I love you."

She saw hurt in his eyes. Hurting him was the last thing she wanted to do. "Why can't we keep seeing each other? Live together?"

He scowled and stepped back from her. Frustration was snowballing into anger. Turning away, he looked at the unopened champagne bottle. He was alert enough to his own feelings to know that if he didn't control them then he'd say things that he'd regret. "Answer one question," he challenged, facing her again. "Do you love me?"

Her throat felt so dry she could barely swallow. Desperately she wanted to believe that he was different from the others. Was that what her mother had felt all those times before she married? Hope. Hope that just one man would love her even though she'd be a disruptive force in his life. Yes, she wanted to hope. "Yes," she said passionately. "Yes, I love you."

"Marry me," he insisted, stepping closer.

Jillian felt as if she couldn't breathe. "David—"

"Marry me," he repeated softly.

As if she'd lost all will to stop herself, she stepped into his embrace. "I do love you." She crumbled beneath her own admittance and gave in to the one thought in her mind. "I do want to marry you."

He released a soft laugh then brushed his lips across hers. Not taking his eyes from her, he reached back and grabbed the bottle of champagne.

As he propelled her toward the doorway, Jillian released a giggle stirred as much by anxiousness as his quick act. "Where are we going?"

"To really celebrate."

Chapter Eleven

David squinted against the morning sunlight. It seemed, brighter, he thought as he stared out his office window. Too much champagne and too little sleep? Or twitter pated? he mused and laughed out loud.

"I heard laughter."

David swiveled his chair around.

Matt gave him a hesitant grin. "You're in a good mood."

"Sit down, will you?" David requested.

Matt plopped on a chair. "It's time for the showdown, huh? Good," he said, looking more concerned than he'd sounded. "I've seen every girl I know," he started out with false lightness, "I spent days camping and fishing with some old friends, and I even played handball with my brother. But all I really wanted to do was talk to you."

"I don't suppose you've changed your mind?"

In less than a heartbeat, Matt's voice raised with a challenge. "I don't suppose you have, either."

The last thing David felt like doing was arguing today, but he'd been as much father as brother for too long.

"I don't need your permission, Dave. I just don't want—I just—damn, I don't want bad feelings between us."

"Then don't run away from—"

"From what? School? I'm not running away. I'll finish. But I want a break from it."

David shook his head. "Do you want to end up like him? The old man took a break from his family, too. You may not remember that. He never came back to us."

"And you never forgave him for leaving us, did you?"

Amazed that his brother even had to ask that question, David struggled to rein his anger. "No, I haven't," he answered evenly.

"Neither have I. I remember."

"You couldn't." David sipped the cold coffee in his cup. "You weren't old enough."

"To remember him leaving?" Matt leaned forward and rested his forearms on the desk. "You're right I wasn't. But I remember a lot of things. The whispering. The way Mom was treated. You aren't the only one who never forgave him for leaving."

David scowled more in confusion than anger.

"I do remember," Matt confirmed softly.

"It's hard to live down."

Matt nodded. "Most of all I never forgave him for what he put you and Mom through."

David offered a wry, mirthless smile. "I tried to protect you, make it easier for you and Carolyn."

"I know you did," Matt assured him. "All those years, you and Mom worked so hard to keep the family together. Mom was old before her time. You, too," he added. "You never had fun, did you? You had too many responsibilities."

David knew the truth in his brother's words, and he avoided Matt's stare.

"I want to," Matt said less angrily. "Before I settle down, I want to enjoy life. Try to understand. I don't feel that I have to measure up to some yardstick acceptable to someone who doesn't count."

David's head snapped up. "What does that mean?"

"Stop trying to measure up to Agnes Simpson and her kind."

"Measure . . . ?"

"Don't you know that they don't matter?"

David stilled. Truth did hurt, he mused. He had been doing just that. He had been trying to live down his father's irresponsible actions. He'd forced a rigidness on himself and his siblings to emulate pillars of society. He'd set high standards for all of them to stop the gossip. Little by little, that realization had been sneaking up on him. But had he been happy all those years? Only recently, because of Jillian, had he finally allowed himself to enjoy life.

"Dave?" Matt pushed himself to a stand. "Dave, are you okay?"

"Yeah," he answered softly, looking up and meeting his brother's stare.

"Dave, try—"

"You're right," he cut in.

Matt stood as if frozen. Apprehensive, he gave David a weak smile. "I'm right?"

The uncertainty in his brother's voice touched him. "You deserve to live your own life whatever way you want. So do I. Neither of us is responsible for the kind of man our father was. I'm not like him, and neither are you." He shoved back his chair and then took a step toward him. "You're a pretty smart kid, aren't you?"

Almost hesitatingly, Matt gave him a crooked smile. "Must be my upbringing."

David laughed and yanked him into his arms. "Somehow you managed to keep your head on straight despite it. Do what you want. Find what you want."

"You, too?" Matt pulled back with a worried stare.

"I already have," David answered as a certainty settled within him.

At noon, Jillian drove out to Grover's Pier to meet David. She glanced at her watch and started to stroll toward the lake to keep from pacing. Why was she feeling so nervous? Why was his opinion about the new store so important to her? Was that part of what love was about? she wondered.

Looking up, she saw his car. As she crossed a grassy knoll to meet him, she took a deep breath.

"Hi," he said, rounding the front of the car.

Accepting the caress of his lips across her cheek, Jillian slipped her arm around his waist and looked down at the newspaper that he'd set on the hood of his car. "What's that for?"

The wind whipped at the edges of the paper. "Riley made the headlines," he said, setting his palm on the newspaper.

"I didn't read this morning's paper. What does it say about him?"

"That he was arrested."

"And he needs a lawyer?"

David scowled. "Not me."

"Oh, good, I was afraid you might do something terribly noble."

"Dumb would be a better word."

"You're never dumb." She looked over his shoulder at the building. How would he view it? He had such a practical eye. "I should prepare you. The building does need a little paint. But I love the natural wood. And I have to get a few lights and new display tables. And there are a few repairs," she paused in her nervous rambling as they slowly walked toward the future site of the Stargazer.

Nothing prepared him for the building that she'd been so pleased with. It was the Grover's Pier shack.

She brushed back hair that had been tossed forward by the wind. Her eyes laughing, she smiled at him. "I have so many plans for it."

Years ago, when most of the land was used for farming, the building had been a barn. Weatherworn and gray, it listed to the left. The sloping roof was patched and slightly sagging. Overgrown grass surrounded it. David looked at the towering willow tree nearby. If a good wind didn't collapse the building, then a bolt of lightning might. In disbelief, he closed his eyes for a second then reopened them, hoping that it didn't look as bad as he thought. It did. "What?" he asked, "what are you going to do with this?"

She smiled because she thought he was teasing. "Isn't it something? It's so charming."

"Until the first rain and the roof falls in."

As he faced her, she saw his disbelief.

"You can't open a business in a dilapidated barn."

"I told you it needed a few repairs."

"Repairs?" He frowned. "I'm not kidding." Couldn't she see it as it was? A rundown building that should have been torn down years ago. "The damn roof will cave in on you."

"No, it won't. David, it has charm. The moment I walked into it, I felt a tranquillity, a—" His eyes narrowed as if he were viewing something alien. She stopped cold. He'd pretended that he understood, accepted her. But would he ever really? That was what had stood between them all this time, what her mother had faced during every marriage. "Use your imagination," she appealed, praying she was misinterpreting his look. "After I make a few repairs—"

"You'll be broke. I can't believe you invested money in this."

"There's nothing wrong with it. You can't see beyond what's in front of you, can you?"

"I don't have that power." The moment he said the words, he regretted them. She visibly tensed and took a step back from him. He damned himself, but getting through to her for her own safety seemed more important than soothing her feelings. "Be practical this time." As she quickly stepped around him and headed toward Andy's car, he didn't try to stop her. "Where are you going?"

"To get my broom like any respectable sorceress would do. And then I'll give a twitch or two," she yelled back without looking at him.

David saw no point in trying to pull his foot out of his mouth. He'd already said too much. As she drove away, he called himself every name for stupid he could think of. With a glance back at the weatherworn building, he swore fluently then headed toward the door of his car.

He didn't remember the drive to her house. He wandered through the shop and then into the kitchen. For a long moment, he watched her yank at one cabinet door and then another. "What are you looking for?"

Anger at herself as much as at him controlled her. For some people love was simple. For the first time in her life, she wished she were ordinary. But she wasn't, and she sensed that this was what her mother must have felt. Life wouldn't be easy for her—or for him. "I'm looking for the tea bags."

When she faced him, he held a palm up toward her in an appealing gesture and then closed the distance between them. That she didn't turn away encouraged him. "I'm sorry." He slid his arms around her waist. "You were excited about the building. I—"

"It needs work," she admitted on a sigh.

He smiled at her understatement. "A little."

Jillian gave him a look that thanked him for not saying more. "Would you like some tea?"

"Coffee." While she knelt in front of a cabinet to search for the tea bags, he lifted the lid of the coffeepot. "There's some left from this morning. And I do make a great cup."

"Modest, aren't you?"

At her teasing, he felt tension flow from him. "Reasonably," he said lightly. When he'd stared at the building, he'd forgotten the dreamer in her. For someone else, it might be a bad investment. But if she believed in something, she'd keep going until she succeeded. In months, she'd have the new shop open. "Don't you have any cookies or—"

"You have a sweet tooth, counselor."

"I know. So is there anything?"

"Oatmeal cookies in—" Jillian stilled. The heavy oppressing darkness descended on her so unexpectedly, so quickly that she swayed from it.

"Where?" he asked, turning around. Her smile was gone. Unblinking, she stared with glazed, distant eyes as if seeing nothing. David approached her slowly. "Jill? Honey, what's wrong?"

"Fire."

"Jill, are you...?" He started to reach for her then stopped himself, uncertain what effect any distraction would have on her. She looked far away despite their closeness. Gone from her eyes was the bright amusement he never seemed tired of seeing. Her face was pale, ghostly. In the restaurant she'd had a similiar look. Yet different. Then she'd been aware of him. Now she wasn't.

"White hair," she said in a soft, frightened voice. "She's falling. Frightened. She can't get up."

Her chest heaved as if fear were gripping her.

"She can't get up," Jillian yelled. "Fire. Smoke. There's—" Breathing heavily, she squeezed her eyes tight. The image grew clearer. Her eyes snapped wide with alarm. "Lillian. It's Lillian."

David remained frozen to the spot for a long moment. With an uncertainty that was alien to him, he touched her hand. It was icy.

"It's Lillian," she screamed. As if he wasn't there, she pushed past him.

David didn't think. Before she reached the door, he caught her arm. "Where are you going?"

Frantically she twisted to break free. "Lillian's in trouble."

The desperation in her voice made him tighten his grip on her arm. "You can't rush over there," he warned. "She'll have you arrested. For God's sake, Jill, you can't—"

He wasn't listening. He wasn't believing, she realized, yanking her arm free from his grasp. "I take chances in life, David. I have to."

A dozen emotions filled him when he reached the doorway and watched her dash down the stairs and across the lawn. Anger, frustration, concern. Mostly isolation. But only one rational thought took root in his mind. He couldn't let her rush into that house. Charging after her, he told himself that he had to stop her, for her own good. If he didn't, Agnes would have the ammunition she needed to trump up some kind of charge against her. Harrassing her neighbor. Hell! Breaking and entering wouldn't be hard to claim, David realized. He could hear Agnes screaming, "witch." And he'd be marked with some saner term like accomplice.

He was two strides behind Jillian when she reached the door. He had no choice. He ran in after her. The moment he did, he smelled the smoke. "Jill!" At no response, panic filled him. Quickly he circled the living room and dining room. "Jill!"

"Down here."

What seemed like an eternity of seconds passed before he reached the kitchen. As he flung open the basement door, a haze of smoke hit him. Though halfway up the basement stairs, Jillian was struggling with the woman who was leaning against her. Her hair straggled, fear still in her eyes, Lillian clung to her.

"She twisted her ankle on the bottom step," Jillian told him between coughs.

"Get out," he ordered, scooping Lillian into his arms.

Steps ahead of him, Jillian raced to the telephone.

When he reached the doorway in the kitchen, she was already giving Lillian's address to the fire department.

David stood on Jillian's front lawn and watched the firemen rerolling hoses.

From the crowd gathered on the sidewalk and in the street, he heard Cornelia's familiar voice. "I'm glad she didn't lose her lovely home."

Iris linked her arm with Cornelia's. As they strolled away from the crowd, she spoke softly. "The fire was contained in the basement."

Both women glanced at Jillian. Standing beside David, she remained still as if frozen to the spot. Her face pale, her eyes were riveted on Lillian's home.

"Jillian saw," Iris whispered to her friend.

Even her friends made her sound like some alien creature, someone set apart from the normal, David thought, as anger churned inside him. She wasn't different. She wasn't strange.

As he shifted to look at her, Jillian braced herself for the moment when his eyes met hers, but she wasn't prepared for the confusion she saw. His thoughtful stare was unnerving. If he married her, his life wouldn't be normal, she reminded herself. Never ordinary. There would be some bad moments. Was he just beginning to realize that? "It scares you, doesn't it?"

"I don't understand it. I may never understand it," he admitted honestly. She looked so controlled, so still. He was used to her animation, to her constant movement. Was this a way of protecting herself? he wondered. From what? From whom? Him? He couldn't blame her. He wasn't any more sure of himself than she was. But he knew what he felt for her. He knew what he needed at the moment. His hand closed over hers. The warmth was there. Always there, he told himself. That never changed. She could attempt to hide it behind a stiff protective mask, but he knew her warmth; he'd felt it consume him.

"I'm a risk you won't like taking, David."

"I don't know about that." Without a word, he slipped his arms around her and pulled her close. "I only know what I feel for you."

She fought the knot in her throat as she buried her face in his shoulder. The arms that wrapped around her offered her strength, the hand stroking her cheek relayed a gentleness she already knew. He represented something she'd never considered wanting. Security. Predictableness. Stability. They were as elusive to her as psychic images were to him. Could he ever truly accept the visions or their unsettling effect on their life together? she wondered. Could any man? "David, it won't work. We both know that." She drew away from him. "You want to play life safe," she reminded him in a voice huskier than usual. "I know some risks are necessary. I can't avoid them." Tears threatened to spill. She held them back, her eyes locking with his. "It's no good."

"What's no good?"

"Marriage."

He needed a moment to catch his breath. Only one thought crossed his mind. He couldn't let it end like this. "What are you talking about?"

Tears streaked her cheeks, and an ache knotted her throat. She swallowed hard against it. "We can't get married."

"Don't say—"

She cut him off. "It won't work!"

"You think that I'll hurt you?" he demanded, unable to find a thread of patience.

"No!" She touched his cheek lightly. "I know you won't mean to. But in the end, you will." She took a painfully hard breath. "And I'll hurt you," she said on a whisper, backing away. She whirled around before he could stop her, before she allowed her heart to change her mind.

Chapter Twelve

David told himself that every man got rejected at some time or another. Rejection he could handle. The hurt gnawing at him was harder to deal with. Pride pushed him through the following day. If she didn't want him enough to give their love a chance, then he wouldn't beg.

Coming out of the bedroom, he heard his brother whistling. For Matt's sake, he would shove aside his personal turmoil for the time they had left together.

As he entered the kitchen, Matt stopped whistling but continued to sprinkle cleanser in the kitchen sink.

When had his brother ever willingly cleaned up anything before? David mused. "When did you get domestic?"

"When did you ever sleep so late?" Matt shot back before he placed the towel on a rack attached to the side of the cupboard. The back of his hand brushed the red scarf hanging from a hook.

David felt the ache resurfacing and turned away.

More attuned to him than David expected, his brother asked in a curious tone, "I'm dying to know before I leave." He fingered the scarf. "Who does this belong to?"

"It's supposed to be good luck."

"Is that so?" Matt nodded with his head and prodded, "That still doesn't answer my question."

"Jillian Mulvane."

Matt looked puzzled. "Her whole family was kind of weird, weren't they?"

Though hours had passed, David still couldn't get those moments from yesterday at Lillian's house out of his mind. He didn't believe in psychic phenomena. He didn't believe in anything that Jillian did. Yet he couldn't come up with a reasonable explanation for what had happened. "Have you ever met her?"

Matt shook his head.

His brother had a lot to learn about life. But then so did he. "Then you don't know her."

Exaggeratingly Matt tiptoed around him.

David gave him a halfhearted grin, but the hurt was too fresh for him to talk about her. "When's your flight?" he asked with a glance at the clock.

"Tired of me already?"

"Just come back soon."

"I will." Matt paused and stood awkwardly before him. "I know that you'd rather I didn't do this—" He released a heavy sigh. "I won't do anything to make you ashamed of me."

David circled his brother's neck with an arm and tugged him close. "I love you. I want you to be happy."

"Yeah." His brother sent him an embarrassed grin. "Ditto."

As Matt reached for his luggage, David placed a hand on his arm. "I'll drive you to the airport."

"It's an hour's drive. I can take a bus."

"No way."

"I'm not going to argue," Matt said. "What can I send you during my worldwide travels?"

David laughed and opened the door. "Send me a primitive mask from some exotic port."

"Do you collect them?"

"Someone special does." With that one comment, David acknowledged that all the words of denial meant nothing. After having had Jillian in his life, being without her wouldn't be easy.

The following morning, awake before five, David left for the office. Work had always helped him to get through rough times before.

Myra said nothing when she came in at eight. She looked at the thick brew setting in the bottom of the coffeepot, walked over, dumped the hours-old coffee, then brewed a new pot. A half hour later, she strolled in and set letters on David's desk. "They need signing."

In a mechanical manner, David picked up a pen.

"I heard that you turned down the town council position."

He nodded. "When I talked to Agnes the other day, I told her I wasn't interested."

"Why? Isn't that what you've wanted?"

"I'll get it in time without someone pulling strings for me." At her silence, David raised only his eyes from the letter he was signing.

A worried look had settled on her face. "Is something wrong?" she asked with concern. "Is everything with Matt okay?"

For a long moment, David stared thoughtfully at her. "What do you know about Jillian's mother?"

"Know?"

"What was she like?"

She swayed slightly as if rocked by the question. "Did something happen with Jillian?"

David drew a rough breath and leaned back in his chair. "What was her mother like?" he repeated.

Myra dropped to the chair near his desk. "She had flaming red hair, laughing blue eyes and a smile that never stopped."

"She looked like Jillian."

Myra tapped a finger at the edge of a stack of papers to realign them. "That isn't what you want to know, is it?"

"No. Do you know more?"

Her eyes slanted toward him. "I know what I think you want to know about."

"Did you ever see it happen?"

"If you want to know whether I was ever with her when she had a vision, the answer is no."

David set down the pen. "Then how do you know about them?"

"Gwen was a good friend. She told me."

David turned away to hide a skepticism that he didn't understand still having. "Was that enough for you?"

"Oh, I see what you mean." She turned her attention to the coffeepot on his credenza. "No, something happened that made everyone know."

"When was this?"

"Gwen wasn't more than a young girl herself then, maybe thirteen or fourteen. A family was camping on Gulliver Ridge. Their little boy and the family puppy wandered off. The boy couldn't have been more than four. A search party was sent out. They found a boy's jacket in the lake and started searching there." She crossed the room and poured two cups of coffee. "Gwen insisted it wasn't the little boy's. She knew where to find him."

"She *saw* where to find him?" David asked hesitantly.

"Few people believed her at first. But her parents believed. And Gus Mulvane was a grizzly old coot. He kept nagging the sheriff to go look where his daughter had said they should." Myra handed him a cup. "Finally when they did and they found the boy in a cave, they thought Gus, Jillian's grandfather, had kidnapped the boy to make fools of everyone."

David frowned. "They seriously believed that?"

"Yes, they did. There was lynching talk."

"What happened?"

"The boy verified that he'd never seen Gus before. Learning that the boy was heartbroken about his puppy, Gwen went to the boy's mother and told her that her son had dropped his jacket on a bush before wandering into the cave. They found the puppy near the jacket.''

David stared at his framed degrees on the wall. He was a pragmatic man by nature. He believed in facts, not seers. But something had happened the other day. Something he couldn't explain and didn't understand.

''After that, everyone looked at Gwen as if she were spooky.'' She sipped her coffee. ''Are you going to sign those letters?''

''Do you believe Jillian can do the same?''

''According to her Mama, she could. But Jillian fights it. Gwen told me that Jillian could even as a little girl. She didn't want to see. But I guess sometimes it just happens.'' She raised a brow. ''Did something happen?''

David nodded while signing the letters. ''We pulled Lillian out of the house during the fire.''

''Oh, I see. Then everyone will know now, won't they?''

''Why do you say that?''

''The newspapers will grab the story and make a big fuss about what happened.''

''Jillian won't tell them.''

Myra looked over the rim of the cup at him. ''She won't have to. She's Gwen Mulvane's daughter. Everyone will know. And she'll have to learn to live with it.''

He handed her the letters. ''Live with what?''

''She watched her mother face ridicule.'' Myra pushed away from the desk. ''David, people either scoff at it or are frightened of it. Which are you?'' she asked, starting for the door.

''Do I have to be one or the other?''

''You'll have to take a stand sometime.''

He thought that he had. He'd told Jillian that he understood, but had he?

Jillian stood in the middle of the barn and contemplated the rafters draped with cobwebs. She wanted to cry again. Cobwebs could be swept away, but the ache inside her heart wouldn't ease up.

She fought her weakness. She had to pick up the pieces of her life, pretend she'd never known David's love, and go on. After working the previous day from dawn until nearly midnight cleaning the Grover's Pier building, she should have been too tired to think. But late at night, even physically exhausted, she hadn't been able to ignore the emptiness in her heart. Memories of David had haunted her as if she'd been cursed.

Why couldn't she forget him? she scolded herself, shivering as a chill swept over her. She stood at the door of her new store and stared up at the sky. The late afternoon sun disappeared behind a heavy gray cloud. More rain, she guessed and whirled around, smacking a broom at a cobweb that was stretched like a lacy curtain from a loft to the double wood door.

Jillian brushed back her hair with a hand. The sound of distant thunder announced the oncoming storm. Looking up, she eyed the roof. ''I hope it's stronger than it looks,'' she murmured to herself. The building was a risky buy. David was right. But people took risks in life. He wouldn't take any, ever. He needed his life predictable and free of scandal. With her, he'd never have such a life. He'd have to defend her sometimes. He'd have to ignore the ridicule. Love wasn't enough. For her mother, for her, a love far stronger than normal was needed.

Sweeping hay into a pile, she swallowed hard. The burning sensation of tears grew stronger. She stopped in the middle of the room and leaned on the broom. She'd seen the look in David's eyes after the fire. He hadn't wanted to hurt her, but he'd been struggling with his own disbelief. She didn't want to be hurt like her mother had been. She didn't want to believe that she had love, and then learn later that it had never existed. Most of all she didn't want to hurt him, she realized, closing the door behind her.

The patter of rain drew David's attention away from the draft of a will and the codicil Myra had just typed.

"Can I bother you again?" Myra asked from the doorway.

David gave her a wry grin. "You usually don't ask."

"This isn't a usual day, is it?" she asked, zeroing in on his mood. She crossed the room and plopped the newspaper on his desk. Again, she said nothing as she stood before his desk.

David glanced at the headline and then skimmed the article about Riley.

Myra tapped the newspaper with a finger. "Ever since Riley's arrest, the newspaper has been milking the story."

David nodded.

"Every relative he has, including Agnes, is getting print space."

David breezed over the section about William Simpson's brief marriage to Gwen Mulvane before his tragic death in a hotel fire. "Agnes must be gritting her teeth," David said.

"I find some pleasure in the woman's discomfort. She's done more than enough damage to other people in her lifetime."

He turned the page and stared at the story about the fire at Lillian's house. Because it had happened days ago, he'd never expected to see the story in print.

"The newspaper gave the story a big spread, didn't it?"

"Yeah." The fuzzy photo showed the fire truck and the crowd of onlookers. Adjacent to the photograph was a smaller one of Jillian and him standing in front of her house. Quickly David read the article. His eyes slowed down as he reached one paragraph.

Over his shoulder, Myra read, "Thanks to neighbor Jillian Mulvane and Lakeside lawyer David Logan, Lillian Hilden escaped unharmed. Mulvane, owner of the Stargazer, a shop featuring astrological charts and crystal balls for the avid fortune-teller, was seen by a neighbor rushing into the house before smoke was even visible."

David didn't read on. He didn't have to. Neither would anyone else. The lines between the printed ones were filled with speculation and suggestion. He felt a tightness building in his chest for her. She was so vulnerable. So fragile. So susceptible to being hurt. So defenseless. Was she frightened? He couldn't blame her. She'd seen her mother hurt over and over again. And when he'd had a chance to prove he wasn't like the rest, that he understood, that he could accept her, he'd failed.

Even though he'd stood beside her and had witnessed that moment when a window was opened to her alone, he'd struggled with doubts, had searched for a reasonable explanation. Second sight was like faith. It required unquestionable belief. It was something, he realized now, that she'd never be able to share with him. But love didn't have conditions. She didn't have to carry the burden of some distorted shame by herself. Was it that shame, not a lack of love, that had made her turn her back on him?

David leaned back in his chair. Was that why his father had run? He'd needed them to love him no matter what had happened. Had he, too, felt that the ridicule and shame he'd brought to his family had put love out of his reach? David felt the ache inside him intensify. He swallowed hard against the constriction in his throat. He couldn't tell his father that they'd never stopped loving him, but Jillian—

Thunder rumbled overhead. David glanced out the window. The storm raged outside, but the one within him was finally gone.

Walking toward home, Jillian raised her chin to let the rain pelt her face. If only it could cleanse the pain inside of her, she mused. David had brought something into her life that she'd never expected: the reality of love. It wasn't always wonderful. It didn't always make a person feel happy. It took hard work and understanding.

By the time she stood in the kitchen and was hunting for candles, the howling wind promised to play havoc with the power lines. As lightning cracked louder, she jumped slightly and looked up. The moment she did, she remembered the last storm. The leaky roof. David. Don't, she warned herself. Don't think about him. Keep busy. Check the attic. Do something but don't remember the wonderful days or the warmth and passion of the nights.

The floor creaked beneath her feet as she walked toward the attic ladder. As she pushed up the hatch, she could hear the rain pounding hard and steady on the roof. Swinging the flashlight up, she surveyed the boards and rafters. Unlike the last time, she heard no distinct plopping of water on the floor. She stood for a moment and waved her flashlight around the room with its pitched ceiling. A smile slowly came to her face as she stared at a blue-flowered lamp her mother had had in her bedroom.

Near the lamp was a trunk her grandmother had brought with her from Ireland. Her mother considered it an heirloom. Jillian knelt down, brushing away the cobwebs, and ran a hand over the scrolled edge of the trunk before lifting the lid. A folded lace tablecloth covered an old photograph. It was her grandparents' wedding picture, sepia-toned and fading.

Outside, the wind whipped against the house, lightning pointed daggers toward the earth, and thunder roared threateningly. But as she touched each article in the trunk, a feeling of serenity drifted over her.

Setting the photographs aside, she beamed the flash-light at her mother's high-school yearbook. What had been her hopes and dreams then? Jillian wondered. As she fanned the pages, slips of paper slid onto her lap.

Jillian unfolded them one at a time: a marriage license to husband number three, a dance keepsake, a love letter. She held the flashlight closer to read the writing. It was masculine and exact. Jillian flipped over the paper then stilled at the signature. William.

Jillian held the letter tight. Tears came without warning. She held them back until they turned into sobs. Why had she never known? she wondered. Why hadn't her mother told her? Why had she assumed that Jillian would know that love was within her grasp? As she let the tears flow, the paper crinkled beneath her fingers. She'd gone through her life be-lieving love wasn't possible, not forever love. "Oh, David," she whispered.

David rapped on the front door then tried the knob. As he wandered through the room, the silence dis-turbed him. He was trained to be controlled. But he couldn't calm nerves. Where the hell was she? he wondered while searching the rooms. Reaching the kitchen, he stared up at the ceiling and released a mirthless laugh. "Okay, Morgana, now what do I do? Where is she?"

As if in answer, a thump resounded overhead.

For a long moment, David stood on the top rung of the ladder and stared at her. With dusk, the attic was cast in a ghostly gray darkness. Her face was pale, her shoulders slumped. As he saw her tears, an ache rippled through him. "Jillian." Though he spoke softly, she gave a start as if he'd yelled at her. He went to her, not thinking about anything except that she needed him. During the drive to her house, he'd made a vow that he'd always keep. If she needed him, he'd be there for her. Unconditional love wasn't easy to give. He'd already let his father down. He'd never make that mistake again.

At his reassuring touch on her hand, Jillian let him slide the letter from her fingers. Desperately she searched for something to say. David, she now realized, had more courage than she did. Unlike her, he hadn't been afraid to take the greatest risk in life. "It's a letter from William to Mama," she said, her voice cracking. "I know now that Mama had been terribly confused and unhappy after his death, because—" She swallowed hard as her throat constricted again. "She loved him. And he loved her."

"You read that in the letter?" David asked, feeling helpless to ease the agony he heard in her voice.

Through blurry vision, she stared at her father's handwriting and nodded. "And he truly believed in her. Mama had warned him that danger awaited. In his letter to her, he wrote that he'd heeded her warning and wouldn't drive home. She didn't need to be fearful of an accident."

"He died in a hotel fire on that trip, didn't he?" David said while he struggled to understand the full meaning of his own words.

"Yes," she answered softly. "She'd seen his death and had tried to warn him. But she hadn't known exactly how it would come." As if her mother were near, Jillian felt her pain. "How frightening for her."

David tightened his arm around her shoulder. There would be more moments like this. And moments when she'd see beyond what was visible. Moments when he'd feel just as helpless to comfort her.

"My mother's marriages hadn't failed because of her 'gift.' Despite her advice of never looking back, she'd never forgotten my father. That's why the other marriages failed." She drew a hard breath, aware how much that revelation would change her life. "I need you," she whispered. "Just as Mama needed him. I need someone who stands firmly on the ground. I'd believed marriage for my mother, for me, would never last. I wanted a guarantee that you'd understand, because I thought that none of her husbands ever had. But that isn't true." At the stroke of his hand on her arm, she drew back to look at him again.

"I didn't understand." He frowned with the admittance. "Not really. I didn't believe before." He tightened his embrace. "I won't hurt you," he promised softly. "Ever."

She shivered at her own foolishness. "Do you really still want me?"

He stifled an urge to laugh. "Idiot." Brushing strands of hair away from her cheek, he assured her, "Having you is more important to me than anything else." He raised her up to stand with him. "I understand that there's a part of you I might never really comprehend. But it doesn't make me love you less." He touched her chin, forcing her to look up. "No matter what, you can depend on one thing. I'll be here for you. I'll always love you."

Sighing, she slid her arms around his waist and held him tight. "I love you. But I worry for you. Will the newspaper story about the fire, will it—"

He placed a fingertip to her mouth to silence her. "You made me a hero."

She shook her head. "Don't joke. You know what I mean. People will link us together."

He grinned at her choice of words. "They'd better. David and Jillian Logan," he said in a speculative tone. "Sounds nice."

"Some people will say that you've lost all good sense."

He framed her face with his hands. "Some will think I'm pretty smart."

His mouth closed over hers. The kiss was sweet and filled with the love that she'd longed for. All her life, she'd believed no man would willingly want to share the disturbing quality in her life. The sturdy, strong arms around her offered a promise. David would share it all with her. He'd accept the bad with the good. She clung to him, amazed at the fear in her own mind that had kept love from her. "This isn't some kind of magic trick, is it?"

"Oh, it's some kind of magic, all right," he assured her. "Real-life magic."

As thunder roared above them, Jillian looked up. "No leaks?"

"Not here, but at my new shop, there's—"

"A woman of vision told me that it's wonderful. I'm not much of a Mr. Fix-It, but I can make a few repairs. We'll work on it. For now, let's get out of here," he said with a quick look upward.

She followed him to the ladder. "Storms are becoming my favorite weather."

"I was going to say the same thing. Memorable." On a laugh, he looked back at the dark attic.

"Very memorable." When he didn't move, she nudged him. "Are we going to stay here?" she teased.

David sent her a puzzled frown. "Where's the seamstress's mannequin?"

"The what?"

"The mannequin," he insisted.

"There isn't one up here."

"Jill, I saw—" David cut his words short. "Never mind," he said with a shake of his head and urged her toward the ladder. "Watch your step."

"I'm not walking. I'm floating."

"Crazy woman."

"I'll find some candles. The power is out again." As she reached the bottom of the ladder, she looked up at him. As if frozen, he stood on the ladder, his head inclined questioningly. "What's the matter?"

"It's quiet," he answered before resuming his climb down. When he stood beside her, he smiled. "No thumping."

Jillian curled her arms around his waist. "Aunt Morgana will be quiet now."

"She's gone?"

Jillian shrugged. "I doubt that. But she's a good loser."

"Won't she be bored?"

Jillian smiled with incredulity at the concern she heard in his voice.

His lips curved in an amused half smile. "I was beginning to enjoy having a resident ghost," he admitted. "I'd hate to see her bored."

"Did you have something in mind?" she asked, tilting her head back to see his face better.

David narrowed one eye speculatively. "A daughter or two to keep her busy."

She released a quick, astonished laugh. "Whatever the future brings. We'll have to wait and see it together."

"The three of us," he murmured against her lips.

"The three—"

"You, me and Morgana."

* * * * *

**A compelling novel of deadly revenge and passion
from bestselling international
romance author Penny Jordan**

POWER PLAY

Eleven years had passed but the
terror of that night was something
Pepper Minesse would never
forget. Fueled by revenge against
the four men who had brutally
shattered her past, she set in
motion a deadly plan to destroy
their futures.

Available in February!

Penny Jordan

SILHOUETTE DESIRE™
presents
AUNT EUGENIA'S TREASURES
by CELESTE HAMILTON

Liz, Cassandra and Maggie are the honored recipients of Aunt Eugenia's heirloom jewels...but Eugenia knows the real prizes are the young women themselves. Read about Aunt Eugenia's quest to find them everlasting love. Each book shines on its own, but together, they're priceless!

Available in December:
THE DIAMOND'S SPARKLE (SD #537)

Altruistic Liz Patterson wants nothing to do with Nathan Hollister, but as the fast-lane PR man tells Liz, love is something he's willing to take *very* slowly.

Available in February:
RUBY FIRE (SD #549)

Impulsive Cassandra Martin returns from her travels... ready to rekindle the flame with the man she never forgot, Daniel O'Grady.

Available in April:
THE HIDDEN PEARL (SD #561)

Cautious Maggie O'Grady comes out of her shell...and glows in the precious warmth of love when brazen Jonah Pendleton moves in next door.

**At long last, the books you've been waiting for
by one of America's top romance authors!**

DIANA PALMER

DUETS

Ten years ago Diana Palmer published her very first
romances. Powerful and dramatic, these gripping tales
of love are everything you have come to expect from
Diana Palmer.

In March, some of these titles will be available again in
DIANA PALMER DUETS—a special three-book collec-
tion. Each book will have two wonderful stories plus an
introduction by the author. You won't want to miss them!

Book 1
SWEET ENEMY
LOVE ON TRIAL

Book 2
STORM OVER THE LAKE
TO LOVE AND CHERISH

Book 3
IF WINTER COMES
NOW AND FOREVER

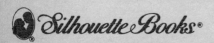 *Silhouette Books*®

Silhouette Intimate Moments®

Available now... it's time for

TIMES CHANGE
Nora Roberts

Jacob Hornblower is determined to stop his brother, Caleb, from making the mistake of his life—but his timing's off, and he encounters Sunny Stone instead. Their passion is timeless—but will this mismatched couple learn to share their tomorrows?

Don't miss Silhouette Intimate Moments #317

Get your copy now—while there's still time!